I'm the One You Need

Rob Matthews

Kenmore, WA

For more information go to: www.fannypress.com

Cover design by Aubrey White

I'm the One You Need

ISBN: 978-1-60381-793-6 (Trade Paper)
ISBN: 978-1-60381-794-3 (eBook)

Produced in the United States of America

Praise for A Cuckold Odyssey

I CAN DO IT BETTER

"A terrific piece of erotica that is hot, sexy, and fun to read. The characters are well developed with depth and complexity. The emotions experienced by the men and women in the story are explored in a way that brings the characters, and the story itself, alive to the reader [….] The erotic scenes are very well done, steamy without being overdone. It's a definite spank bank book, if you're into cuckold/hotwife fiction [….] I highly recommend this for cuckold/hotwife fans."
—Putaine Musings

"Yes, a thousand times yes. I love it when a book goes all mental like that, from the point of view of a character (with a little insight from the writer), and we go deep down the rabbit hole inside someone's head[….] I dropped right into this book like a comfortable chaise lounge, never getting lost, and never needing to read the book one – and that is the hallmark of a writer who knows how to pick up on a story while keeping a newcomer perfectly informed, and also very nice work[….] Recommended strongly for those wishing to dive deep into the hows and whys of cuckolding."
—Sylvia Storm, eRead Erotica Reviews

COME HOME WITH US

"It goes above cuckolding, gets into what it is to love and have a relationship, and goes there. It is really, once you get into it, an amazing piece of work…. Do I recommend this? Yes. Strongly so."
—Sylvia Storm, eRead Erotica Reviews

"*Come Home With Us* tells the story of a VERY modern marriage. Fantasies are the spice of a couple's life, but what happens when Rob and Tina take their fantasies one step further? What if Rob truly becomes a cuckold? Hot sexual escapades are a big part of the fun here, but underneath the marital covers are secrets that could change everything. What happens when they come to light? Those were the questions I savored while reading this cuckolding page-turner."
—Alex Hathaway, author, *Education of a Cuckold*, *From Housewife to Cuckoldress*, and *My Husband's Adventures*

WE MAKE OUR OWN RULES

"One thing I truly love about Mr Matthews books is that not only is he a terrific writer of erotica, he is also a fantastic story teller. When I pick up one of his books I know it's going to be hot and sexy, but what is even better is that I know he is going to tell me a great story. I know he is going to create characters who have depth and complexity; characters that I will care about, love, or even hate. His stories are interesting and entertaining as well as being steamy, and We Make Our Own Rules does not disappoint in any way."
—Shaun Putaine, Putaine's Musings

Also by the Author

Black and Blue

A Cuckold Odyssey series

Come Home With Us

I Can Do It Better

We Make Our Own Rules

Chapter One

~

I WAS AT A SHOW that was supposed to be erotic. The women I on stage were nude apart from blank-face masks. I realized one of the women was my wife and rushed onto the stage to rescue her.

That had to be a dream, right?

And now I was in bed with two naked women. But I was a cuckold. *Bulls* got to share a bed with beautiful women. *Cuckolds* were lucky if they were allowed to sit on a chair and watch.

Definitely a dream.

My back was against the wall. Tina's hair tickled my face and her ass was pressed into my crotch. Her body was curled into a C-shape, giving Charlotte a hollow to sleep in. My wife's hand rested on Charlotte's thigh while my arm was around both of them like a safety belt. Lifting my head, I saw my suit jacket, which I'd wrapped around Tina as I'd hurried her off the stage. Lying beside it was the mask that had hidden my wife's face and tried to drain her of personality.

It looked like it had all really happened.

I'd woken with an impressive erection, which might have been down to the naked women, but probably meant I needed to pee. I wormed my way to the bottom of the bed and managed to get out without waking them. Before going into the bathroom, I picked up the mask. I didn't want Tina seeing it again but, as it was plastic, I couldn't rip it up and flush it. I pushed it to the bottom of the wastepaper basket.

After I'd finished on the toilet, I closed the lid to deaden the noise of the flush, but it still broke the silence like the roar of a mighty river. Charlotte and Tina were blinking and scratching themselves awake as I came back into the bedroom. Realizing she had her hand on another woman, Tina started and sat up. 'Good morning,' said Charlotte.

'Morning,' replied Tina, shortly.

I thought they could smooth over any awkwardness by picking up where they'd left off the night before. Tina had licked another woman's cunt for the first time, and Charlotte had returned the favor. I'd have been more than happy if they'd wanted to do that again. But Tina suddenly put her right arm across her breasts. She looked around for her clothes, but I hadn't thought to pick them up as I'd bundled her out of the theater.

'Er … Charlotte,' I said, gesturing toward Tina.

'Give me a minute,' said Charlotte. She put on a t-shirt and a pair of sweat pants, and left the room.

'Raiding lost property,' I told Tina. 'Her own clothes would be too small for you.'

Five minutes later, Charlotte came back with a red pleated skirt and a pair of white basketball boots. 'I figured you wouldn't want to wear someone else's underwear. And I didn't find any tops that would fit you. But I've a long black nightshirt. It'll be a regular t-shirt on you.'

Tina didn't look too thrilled with her new clothes, but she put them on. I got into my tuxedo and suit trousers, stuffing the bow-tie into my jacket pocket so I didn't look too much like I was staggering home after an all-night party.

'The kitchen will be open,' said Charlotte. 'It's usually pretty busy on Sunday morning, but I can try to rustle up some breakfast, if you want.'

'We have to go and pick up our dog,' said Tina.

I thought she emphasized the words "we" and "our" more than she had to. I hoped she wasn't giving Charlotte the message: *We're* going back to *our* life as a married couple—I don't know what *you're* going to do.

Charlotte tried—unsuccessfully—to look like she didn't care what we did. 'Okay … well … if you could find a way of getting the shirt back to me some time ….'

I gave Charlotte a hug and said, 'Thank you so much for everything.'

Charlotte put her arms around Tina's waist and said, 'Last night was great.'

It seemed Tina didn't know how to respond so, falling back on common courtesy, she mumbled, 'Thank you for letting us stay.'

Charlotte's eyes were red. I was sure she'd start crying as soon as the door closed behind us. I couldn't stand it and asked, 'Are you free this evening?' She nodded. 'Come over to our place for dinner.' I picked up the pen that was lying by the bed and looked around for some paper. Charlotte held out her left hand and I wrote our address on the back of it.

Tina and I went out. As we started along the corridor, Tina asked, 'What are you doing, Rob?' Her tone wasn't angry, just curious.

'How do you mean?'

'You and I have to talk. Is this the time to be hosting dinner parties?'

'That girl's been a good friend to me,' I said, firmly. 'There's no way I'm going to abandon her.'

Tina shook her head, but didn't say any more. I led her to the service elevator. It was a route I'd taken many times over the past weeks, but it felt strange to have Tina with me in the place where I'd always been with Charlotte. It reminded me of when my mom visited my school: she looked out of place in this environment that wasn't hers. 'Where are we?' asked

Tina. She'd been so dazed the night before that she hadn't paid attention to where we were going.

'A hotel in town,' I replied. 'Charlotte's one of the receptionists. You'll recognize it when we get out.'

As soon as we stepped onto the street, she said, 'All this time, you were walking distance away.'

'Yes,' I said, in a neutral voice. 'Are you okay in those shoes?'

'They're a bit too big, but it should be fine.'

'Try not to be hit by a car. It'll be embarrassing if you have to go to ER with no underwear.'

'I'll do my best.'

It was a cold November morning, so I took my jacket off and put it around Tina's shoulders. We didn't say any more as we walked home. The first thing I noticed as I opened our front door was the smell of Adam. It was like my wife's lover was still there, lingering in the air.

It was only eight o'clock. 'We can't fetch Boris yet,' said Tina. 'No sane person gets up before ten on a Sunday.' So her assertion that we had to rush off to pick up our dog wasn't entirely accurate.

'I'll make some coffee,' I said.

The kitchen also bore the signs of someone else having lived in our house. The coffee pot wasn't where I normally kept it. The apples in the bowl on the counter weren't the sort I'd have chosen. There was a make of wine in the fridge that Tina and I didn't usually drink.

Going into the den, I found Tina on the couch. She'd left the drapes closed and turned the light on. Sitting beside her, I poured us each a large mug of coffee. After a silence that went on too long, I said, 'So, you're a lesbian now.'

I watched her face, willing a smile to spread over it. Eventually it did, and she broke into a laugh. 'Just when you think you're too old to try anything new,' she said. She took a sip of coffee and looked thoughtful for a moment. 'And there was a strict no-alcohol-backstage rule last night, so I can't blame it on booze. I got caught up in the moment.'

'Did you enjoy it?'

'Yes … yes, I did,' she replied. 'Charlotte's very pretty and, damn, that girl knows how to eat pussy.'

'Better than me?' It was a question I'd asked many times in my role as cuckold.

'About the same, I'd have said.'

I reflected that, if Tina had been with another man the night before, she'd have taunted me mercilessly about how I could never dream of pleasuring her the way he did.

'Would you have enjoyed it more if Charlotte had been a six foot guy with a hairy chest and an eight inch dick?'

'I'd have enjoyed it in a different way,' she said, diplomatically. 'I think I'll always be mainly attracted to men, but ….' She paused and looked at me. Did I see a ghost of her wicked grin? 'But I think I'd regret it if I didn't explore the girl-on-girl world a *little* more.'

Her words made my cock stir, but I ignored it and asked, 'Why were you so uncomfortable when we woke up this morning?'

She put her chin in her hand and spoke thoughtfully. 'It was reality hitting me in the cold light of day. There's been a lot to take in, babe.' I nodded, knowing exactly what she meant. 'One minute, I'm parading before a crowd of men like I'm at a slave auction. Next thing I know, I'm back with my husband and I find he's shacked up with Morticia's little sister. How did *that* happen, Rob?'

'She took me in when I needed somewhere to stay.'

'Why?'

I shrugged. 'It shouldn't have worked. She likes horror films, romantic comedies, and pop divas. But, when we started talking … it felt right. I realized I'd made a new friend.'

She gave me a look that was both stern and fearful. 'And that's all you were—friends?'

'We *are* friends.' I didn't want any suggestion that Charlotte belonged to my past.

Tina sighed as if I were being pedantic. 'You know what I

mean.'

I took a mouthful of coffee, and pretended to choke on it to buy some time. I knew I loved Charlotte, but I wasn't sure what sort of relationship we had, or what sort I wanted. 'Well, as you discovered, Charlotte's largely a lesbian.'

Tina looked skeptical. 'I've never heard anyone chanting, "We're here! We're largely queer!" '

'What were you saying about wanting to explore the girl-on-girl world a little more?'

'Yes, all right,' admitted Tina.

'Charlotte says we're all gay and we're all straight, to differing degrees.'

'Even Liberace had his hetero moments?'

'If Charlotte's to be believed.'

'And did she have any such moments with you?' asked Tina, insistently. She wanted to know if I'd broken the rules. Tina was a hot wife and I was a cuckold. We weren't swingers. An important rule was that she could have sex with anyone she fancied while I had to remain faithful.

It would have been easy to lie, and that would have made the rest of the conversation more comfortable. But if both Charlotte and Tina were going to be in my life, the truth would come out eventually. 'I've never fucked her,' I said. 'And one of us always changed in the bathroom, so I didn't see her naked until last night. And when I showed you how to lick her, that was the first time I did anything like that with her.'

'You get a free pass for last night. You're saying before that you were like brother and sister?'

'Not exactly. There was a physical side to our relationship.'

'Define,' said Tina, suspiciously.

'She … asked me to spank her once.'

Tina's eyes widened. 'And did you?'

'Yes, but it was in the dark, so I didn't see her ass.'

'I'm not sure that makes it better,' she said, pursing her lips.

'And one time she teased me about what you might be doing with Adam.'

'Did she make you cum?'

'She loaded the gun, but I pulled the trigger myself.' I realized that could be ambiguous, so I clarified, 'She's never touched my cock.'

Tina was silent for a while, processing what she'd heard. 'I suppose it could have been worse,' she said, slowly.

'Yes, it could. And, lest we forget, you weren't sticking to the rules, either. You've always said, "Love the cuck, not the stud." '

'I *am* sorry, babe. Adam got inside my head. If you're having great sex with someone who knows what you're thinking, it can feel a lot like love.'

Shaking my head, I said, 'He didn't know what you were thinking. He'd read a couple of psychology books and maybe some magician had taught him mind-reading tricks.'

'Perhaps, but he was good at it. How do you think he persuaded me to appear in the show?'

'I was going to ask. What voodoo did he work there?'

'As always, he knew which buttons to push. He told me I could be in the show if I wanted, but he didn't think I could compete with the younger girls. It made me determined to prove I was more than a match for those bitches with their gravity-defying tits and butts like little apricots. I wanted to hear the loudest cheer when *I* came on. I needed a room full of men to want *me* more than anyone else on the stage.' She looked sadly at the opposite wall. 'The mask was a surprise, though. They told us it was a challenge. If no one could see our faces, we'd have to project ourselves through our bodies.'

'And I thought they were saying a woman's personality doesn't matter so long as she has great tits and ass.'

A tear ran down her cheek. 'That could have been it.'

I put a supportive hand on her leg. After a moment, her eyes hardened and she pushed my hand away. 'I'm mad at you for bailing on me, Rob. It would never have happened if you'd been here.' I found this hard to believe. Adam had persuaded her to do many things, and my presence had never stopped him. 'I was going to a scary place. You made me go there alone.'

I felt my anger rising. Breathing deeply to keep calm, I said, 'What do you mean, "scary place"? You weren't going into hospital. You wanted to explore parts of your sexuality. Wherever you were going, it was entirely your choice, so it's hard to feel much sympathy for you. And you weren't alone. I asked you to decide between Adam and me. I lost the vote.'

'Mm,' she said, which I took as a grudging admission that I might have a point. I couldn't help comparing her reaction to the time she'd come home after moving in with Steve, her first lover. She'd admitted how stupid she was to think anyone could take my place and pretty much begged me to have her back. The sound, 'Mm,' did not measure up to her previous show of contrition. 'Do you want to know why?' she asked. Before I could answer, she added, 'I can show you.'

'How?'

'Take your clothes off.'

'What?'

'Come on, Rob. What's the worst that could happen?' The last time I'd taken my clothes off in this house, I'd ended up with toothpaste stinging my cock and balls. Nevertheless,I stood up and took off the tuxedo and suit trousers. Slipping off my shorts, I sat beside her. She sat up straighter and looked at me with a critical eye. 'I'm going to tell you everything that's wrong with your body.'

'Why?'

'You'll see.' She looked down with a smirk. 'Your little friend already likes the idea.' My cock was semi-erect. 'I should warn you, I'm going to be cruel with my comments.' My cock immediately grew to its full size. It wasn't the first time my cock had given enthusiastic approval to something I wasn't sure about.

She examined my face, like an art dealer evaluating a painting. 'Your face isn't too bad,' she said, at last. 'I could do better. Hey, I *have* done better. Steve was better-looking than you, with his dark hair and deep brown eyes. But we'll give your face a pass mark.' Her gaze travelled south and she prodded my shoulders and arms. 'You didn't go to the gym much while you were with Charlotte. Getting flabby.'

There was something in this. I'd never seen Charlotte do any exercise. She was worryingly thin, despite spending most evenings with a can of beer in one hand and a pack of M&Ms in the other. I know I could have stopped off at the gym on my way back to the hotel after work but, somehow, this had never happened.

Putting her hand on my chest, Tina said, 'But here's where the real problems start. I've gotten used to real men with hairy chests. You don't have a single hair on yours, not even any peach fuzz. Are you a man, Rob? Or a flat-chested woman? It's hard to tell.' She moved to my belly. 'Fewer pies; more sit ups,' was all she had to say there. She passed over my cock and balls. I knew they weren't going to have a free ride, but she was saving them for last. 'Your legs are hairy, but what good are hairs down there? If we could transplant them to your chest, you'd almost be a man. Your thigh and calf muscles should be bigger and more defined. But we'll give your legs a C minus— I'm feeling generous.' She put her hands on my balls. 'But here's where you really fail.' She squeezed them and dug her nails into the delicate skin. I flinched involuntarily, but was turned on enough to enjoy the pain. 'I love big balls. I like licking them and rolling them between my fingers and thumb. With you, I don't have anything to get hold of and have a good time with. I want to feel a man's balls smacking into me while I'm being fucked. Yours are … nothing.' She gave me a sympathetic look. 'Did you lose your balls in an accident? Is that why you have an empty sack?' She paused and squeezed my balls again, harder this time. Despite what she'd said, she seemed to be having a good time with them. She moved her hand up and wrapped it around my cock. She caressed it gently for a few seconds and then pulled it toward her with such a sharp tug that I cried out. Going back to rubbing it gently, she said, 'As for this …. When I first saw it, I thought it was okay. But I was young and naïve back then. I didn't know what a penis was supposed to be like. Kieran had the cock I deserve. Steve and Adam didn't have cocks which were much *bigger* than yours, but they were so much *better*. The job of a cock is to get inside a woman and fuck her until she can't take any more. Yours shoots off in less than a minute. How does it make you feel, Rob? Your cock can't do its job. Sorry, it's not good enough for me anymore.' She stopped and smiled at me, showing this part of the game was over. My cock was still standing up, hard and straight. She gave it another tug—not so hard this time—and said, 'You obviously like it when I talk like that.'

'I do,' I said. 'But I'm not sure how it relates to what we're discussing.'

'All will be revealed.' As if to prove the truth of this, she stood up and pulled the t-shirt over her head. It took her a moment to work out the unfamiliar fastenings on the skirt, but then it fell to the floor. Naked, she sat back on the couch with her legs stretched out in front of her. 'Your turn,' she said. 'What's wrong with my body?'

We'd tried things like this before, and I'd always been bad at it because I could never see anything that needed improvement. I felt I *had to* find fault this time. 'Your tits are too small,' I began. 'I like big breasts I can bury my face in. And you haven't been spending much time in the gym, either. You've lost tone around your stomach and on your legs. And your pussy is—'

'You don't mean any of this, do you, babe?'

'No,' I sighed. 'You look great.'

'And that's why I need someone else.' She put her arms behind her head and looked at the ceiling. 'Maybe I need Adam back.'

I didn't like this idea. 'So your sole ambition now is to find a man who insults your body?'

She frowned. 'Put it like that, it sounds a bit strange.'

'You think?'

'But surely *you* can understand, Rob. I've insulted *your* body and your cock is straining toward the ceiling. And you love it when you watch another man fucking me and I say, "He's *so* much better than you, babe." ' I couldn't deny this. The mere thought of her doing that was making my cock throb even harder, but it was frustrated by having nothing except air to push against. 'I thought it was only men who felt like that. But I've found out I do too. When Steve compared me to the last married woman he'd fucked, it didn't do much for me because I didn't know her. But when Adam compared me to Emma, it drove me wild because she was right before my eyes. I could *see* that what he said was true.' I was about to say something when Tina held up her hand. 'Don't deny it, Rob. I've seen the way you look at her. She is gorgeous. Adam liked to have me and her naked on the bed in front of him.' I took a moment to picture that. Our friend Emma was a black-haired, dark-eyed beauty who oozed sexy sophistication. No man has done enough good in this world to deserve both her and Tina in bed with him. 'And he'd tell me all the ways my body was worse than hers. He gave what amounted to a mathematical proof that her tits were better than mine. And then he fucked her in front of me.'

'So … he *cuckolded* you.'

'Essentially, yes.'

'It's not something you hear much about—female cuckolds.'

'Maybe I'm unique.'

'People will write papers about you—for *The Lancet* or *Fetish World*, I'm not sure which.' I was quiet for a minute, thinking over what she'd said. 'No one knows better than me how powerful a fetish can be,' I said. 'But to risk your marriage over something like that ….'

'I wasn't risking my marriage. I knew you'd be back.' I looked into her eyes and saw something I hated—complacency. She was convinced my love for her was so strong that she could do whatever she pleased and I'd always be there for her at the end. 'And there was more to it than that,' she said. 'Maybe I wasn't really in love with Adam, but I had strong feelings for him. He knew that, and so did Emma. That's what made it so exciting for them to screw in front of me. She grinned at me over his shoulder as he enjoyed her skinny bitch body. The heart-pounding, breathless jealousy was almost unbearable. But, at the same time, it was such a turn-on.' She looked at me and smiled. 'I'm preaching to the choir here, aren't I?'

I was still annoyed, but I nodded. 'Jealous. Angry. Horny. The three cornerstones of cuckoldry.'

'The difference was, after they'd finished, I couldn't claim Adam back by fucking him, because he was spent. But sometimes I was allowed to masturbate.'

'Nice of them to give you permission.'

'You know how these games play out. I sat there, pleasuring myself, while Emma looked at me with a sneer that said, *You use your fingers—I use your man's cock.* And to think, when she first met me, she called me "Goddess Tina." ' She patted the couch we were sitting on. 'And when it was all over, I normally bedded down right here. That's no way to treat a goddess.'

I knew all too well what that was like, but I never thought it would happen to Tina. 'They didn't even let you sleep with them?'

She shook her head. 'Adam preferred to sleep with Emma and Ben.'

'Really?' I was surprised. No offense to Emma's husband, but I couldn't understand why any straight man would prefer to sleep with Ben instead of Tina.

She explained, 'Adam loved the rivalry between me and Emma. But his greatest thrill was always fucking Emma in front of her husband. And afterwards, he liked to watch Emma and Ben cuddle up in bed together like a nice married couple, knowing her pussy was still sore from his cock.' She looked at me, sadly. 'It's why he cooled on me after you moved out, babe. He was interested in us because we were a happily married couple. He wanted to get in the middle and see what he could stir up.' She shook her head. 'I wasn't all that fascinating on my own, so he looked around for another couple. Emma and Ben were perfect for him. For all I know, he's round at their place now.' I saw that complacent look again. 'I love you, Rob, and you love me, which is great, but it means you'll always choose me over anyone else. So I'll never feel that jealousy when I'm with you.'

As I looked at her, sitting back with her hands behind her head, something struck me. 'I wish you had hairy armpits,' I said.

She raised her head and looked at me curiously. 'What? Where did that come from?' Her mouth opened as she realized, 'You want me to be more like Charlotte!'

'Charlotte's armpits are beautiful. They're one of the sexiest parts of her. Yours are … nothing.'

Her eyes flashed. 'You mean it, don't you?'

'Yes, I do,' I said, sincerely.

'You compared me unfavorably to another woman. Someone I know.' She looked at me for a moment, then said, 'Fuck me.'

I've always found sex on the couch to be one of those things that sounds better than it really is. With her half-sitting, half-lying on it, there wasn't enough room for me to kneel between her legs, so I hovered over her, supporting myself with my hands on either side of her head. Tina took hold of my cock and put it at the entrance to her cunt. I pulled myself forward and was able to penetrate her. It was not a comfortable position. For once, I was happy to finish quickly. It was only a few seconds before I pulled out of her. She pointed to her belly. My cock pulsed with relief as I came over my wife. A lot had built up over the past few days and she had a shiny, ivory-colored pool around her belly button. It was good to see *my* semen on Tina again.

I took a couple of tissues out of my pocket and cleaned her up. She nodded. 'I actually felt something there.'

'Good to know.'

Sitting up, she looked at me keenly. 'Did you say you spanked Charlotte?'

'Her ex-girlfriend used to punish her. She wanted to feel

some of that again.'

'I always thought you were too *nice* to spank anyone.' Generally, it's a good thing to be nice, but she said it in a way that suggested *weak*.

'Don't count on it,' I said.

She heard the angry edge to my voice and it seemed to arouse her. Stoking the fire, she said, 'I'm thinking back to the evening when Ben put toothpaste on your junk. I *loved* seeing you like that. It wasn't only your pain that turned me on, but also your humiliation. Have you any idea how ridiculous you looked?' It was less than a minute since I'd cum, but my cock was getting hard again. I wasn't sure I liked what was happening to my relationship with Tina, but if it was turning me into a stud who was always ready for action, I couldn't complain. She bit her lip. 'I guess you're still mad at me for that.'

'Furious,' I assured her.

'I deserve to be punished.'

She stood up and turned around. Kneeling on the couch, she rested her face against its arm and pointed the perfect curve of her ass toward me. It made my cock fully erect again. I hadn't been so virile since I was eighteen. The sight of Tina in this position was so erotic that part of me wanted to forget all this punishment nonsense and just fuck her. I forced myself to remember that there was more to her than a great body. This was the woman who had laughed while I was in pain. She'd chosen another man over me, her husband. She'd made me leave my home.

I wasn't aware of any voluntary movement in my arm. It was like the anger built up inside me until the spank happened by itself. I heard the sound of flesh meeting flesh. I felt the sting on my palm. A hand-shaped red mark formed on the white skin of her right buttock. I spanked her another five times—hitting different places. When both her buttocks were a rosy pink, I remembered the lesson I'd learned from Charlotte about selecting one part of the ass for *serious pain*. I chose the middle of Tina's right buttock. I spanked the same place six times, as hard as I could, then pushed my nails into the sore place and scratched it. By the time I'd finished, it was bright red with a couple of bruises forming. Four red lines were scored into it, with a little blood at the end of two of them.

Adam used to scratch words onto my wife's skin. The nail on my pointing finger was short but, even so, I used it to write two words in shaky capitals.

'What did you write?' she asked, breathlessly.

' "PAIN SLUT." '

She moaned. 'Is that all I am to you now? Your pain slut?'

Kneeling on the couch behind her, I used my thumbs to spread the cheeks of her ass and expose both her holes. I'd have loved to penetrate her tight little asshole, but I didn't want to waste time looking for lube. I stuck my cock into her cunt and laid my chest against her back so I could squeeze her right breast and whisper fiercely in her ear. 'Yes, it's all you are. Next time, I'm not going to use my hand. I'm going to take my belt to you. And when I've finished whipping your ass, I'm going to turn you over, make you spread your legs, and I'm going to use my belt on your—'

I'd cum a few minutes before and I hoped this would make the second time last longer. But my words excited me even more than they did Tina. I clenched the muscles in my groin desperately, but the gates had been opened, and my sperm was only going one way. 'Sorry,' I said, which detracted from the masterful persona I was trying to create.

'Pull out and cum over my ass,' she said.

I aimed at the broken skin, hoping my cum would sting her the way the toothpaste had stung me. There wasn't much this time—a small patch on her right buttock.

She heard me reaching into my pocket for another tissue. 'No,' she said, 'lick it up.' I knew what she was doing. After our foray into male domination, she was reasserting her position as cuckoldress. I didn't like the taste of my semen—or anyone else's—but I accepted it as part of being a cuckold. And I told myself I should relish any opportunity to lick Tina's ass.

I swallowed it quickly and sat up with the familiar feeling of something in the back of my throat I couldn't clear.

Tina turned around and sat down. She winced as her bare ass touched the fabric, and looked at me with a new respect. 'That was a good spanking,' she said, sounding annoyingly surprised. 'Remind me to thank Charlotte when I see her. She's taught you well.' She paused and then asked, 'You were genuinely angry there, weren't you?'

I couldn't deny this, but I could try backpedaling a little. 'Angry at some of the things that have happened ....'

'So, not angry with *me*, at all?'

'Well ....'

'It's okay. If you're going to do things like that, you can be as angry as you want.' She shook her head. 'But I'm sorry, Rob, I still want someone else. I'll always be a cuckoldress. We can't put the cork back in the bottle. And ....'

I sighed. 'Say it.'

'And, although the spanking was great—I loved that—the actual sex still wasn't enough for me.'

'I know.'

'I want someone who's going to spank me until I scream, then fuck me until I cum like a bitch. After that, I'm going to need you there to look after me. That means I'm never going to do anything unless you're right there in the room. Got that, babe? I must have you there every single time.'

It seemed to me I'd heard that song before.

She put her arm around me. 'So let's forget everything that's happened and go back to the way it was. Okay, babe?'

I wondered if this was possible.

Chapter Two

~

AT TEN O'CLOCK, WE drove over to Louise's place. When we rang the doorbell, there was joyful barking from inside. Louise opened the door and Boris almost knocked Tina over, running to me. 'Missed you too, honey,' said Tina, sourly. But Boris had spent only one night away from Tina. He hadn't seen me in nearly a month. I knelt on the path so he could lick my face. I put my arms around him and hugged him. 'Has he been okay?' asked Tina.

'Best dog ever,' replied Louise. 'You guys had breakfast?'

'Not yet,' said Tina.

I stood up. 'Are you okay, Rob?' asked Louise.

'Something in my eye.'

We went inside. When we all had a croissant and a glass of orange juice, Tina and Louise sat on the couch, while I took the armchair. Boris insisted on jumping up. A shaggy black Labrador-based mongrel, he was too large to sit comfortably on one lap, but I wasn't about to tell him to get down. He sat facing me so I could pat his head and rub his chest. Tina asked Louise, 'How are you doing?'

Louise shook her head. 'Not so good. I know it's more than a year since I found out about Nathan, but … it doesn't get any better.'

Louise was a tall, striking woman with ash blonde hair and pale green eyes. But her mouth was down-turned and she had black bags under her eyes.

'Have you seen him?' asked Tina.

'Quite often, actually. He comes round when he needs to pick up bits and pieces. Sometimes, he stays for a drink and we chat away, almost like nothing's happened. I think he wants us to try again but ....' She closed her eyes for a second. 'I can't forgive him for putting me through that moment.'

Tina looked puzzled. 'Moment?'

'I never told you, did I?' Louise took a sip of juice and spoke in a low voice, 'It was Sunday afternoon. He had to go on a business trip and was leaving in half an hour. He had some "work" to do on the computer before he left. After he'd gone, I went on to check my emails and saw he hadn't signed out of his account. I knew I should respect his privacy and log out, but ....' She looked over at me and asked, 'Rob, can you honestly say you wouldn't look at Tina's emails if you had the chance?'

'Wouldn't dream of it,' I said.

Louise snorted. 'Yeah, right. Anyway, if I hadn't peeped, Nathan might be here now. But curiosity overcame my scruples and I found a whole lot of emails between him and this whore called Caitlin.' She spat out the name as if it were the worst possible swear word. 'That was the moment when the bottom fell out of my world. In the first one, she said she was lying in bed, touching herself while she thought about him. I thought maybe they'd met in a chat room or something and were just erotic pen pals.' She gave me a pointed look. 'Which is wrong, whatever men say. E-cheating is still cheating. But it would have been better than anything going on in real-time. Then I saw one that said, "I couldn't wait for the boring meeting to finish, so we could go back to your hotel room and have a much more productive meeting." And another one, "When we finish work on Thursday, why don't you come round to my place for a bite? I have a couple of things which need biting." I'm sure it was her sense of humor he found so irresistible.' A tear welled up in her right eye. Tina reached for her hand and squeezed it. 'A couple of emails had photos attached. Pictures of her—nothing explicit. She's in her twenties—slim, beautiful, with perfect skin.' Her hand tightened around her croissant. 'She could have any man she wanted, and she had to go for mine.'

'I'm so sorry,' said Tina.

'And the thing is, I couldn't stop looking at those damn emails. Even though the first two gave me enough evidence for a watertight case, I kept opening one after another.'

I was familiar with the masochistic yearning for more and more information. Many times, I'd pressed Tina for every detail about what she did with another guy, what they said, and how she felt while they were doing it.

'Then I looked to see if he'd emailed her on special dates,' said Louise. 'Had he contacted his slut on my birthday, our anniversary, Valentine's Day? I also wanted to see if she knew about me. Was she laughing at me? Or, worse, did she feel sorry for me?'

'Did you tell him as soon as you discovered?' asked Tina.

Louise sighed. 'I was going to tear him a new one over the phone, but I thought it would be too easy for him to hang up. I decided to wait until he was here—captive audience. But when he came back, he seemed so pleased to see me and it was kind of nice being with him again. But as it got closer to the time he had to leave, he sensed something was wrong and asked me. I blurted it all out and, of course, he tried to blame me.'

'Well, he is a man,' said Tina.

'He said I shouldn't have been snooping in his emails. Then he told me I was boring in bed.'

'What an asshole.'

'Yes, apparently there's all this kinky shit he's always wanted to try.'

'Like what?' asked Tina.

This didn't seem an appropriate question to ask, and I gave Tina a reproving look. She didn't notice and Louise wasn't fazed. 'Yes, I asked him—for the same reason I couldn't stop looking at the emails. At first, he wouldn't tell me. He said I was too uptight to understand. I wish I'd left it there.' Taking a deep breath, she said, 'Apparently, Caitlin likes being tied up and teased. She also thinks it's perfectly acceptable for a woman to have no privacy. She's happy for him to watch when she's in the shower and even on the toilet. Can anyone explain what's supposed to be sexy about that?'

Tina seemed about to speak, but settled for patting Louise's knee.

With an exaggerated gesture of indifference, Louise said, 'She's welcome to him.' But her eyes were still moist. 'If you see him, give him a kick, will you?' she added.

'With pleasure,' replied Tina. 'Is he still living around here?'

'I think so. Coming over doesn't seem like a big deal so I guess he's not far away.'

'You know what we should do?' said Tina. 'Let's have another girls' night out some time—pick up a couple of hot guys, make us both feel better.' Louise looked surprised and tilted her head toward me in a *You realize he's right here?* way. Tina laughed. 'Don't worry about Rob. If you ask him nicely, he'll tell you the whole story some time.'

Louise gave me a quizzical look, then turned back to Tina. 'I don't want to meet anyone else right now.'

I was worried about Louise. The year before, she'd signed up to dating sites and said she was going to have sex with every man on the planet to get back at Nathan. But now, the fight seemed to have gone out of her.

As we got up to leave, Louise stroked Boris's ears and said, 'You know you can bring him here any time. Even if you're not going anywhere. I mean, if you want a break from him.' He rubbed his head gratefully against her leg and followed us out.

Tina drove while I sat in the back with Boris. 'Poor Louise,' she said, over her shoulder. 'It must have been awful, finding out like that.'

'The first inkling *I* had you might be seeing someone else was when Steve got you on all fours and fucked you in front of me.'

'It was a pretty strong clue,' she agreed. 'Whatever else has happened, Rob, we've always been honest with each other.'

This made me feel guilty. I'd never properly told Tina about having sex with my colleague, Danielle. But I decided this wasn't the time.

After we arrived home, we returned to something like ordinary life. Tina put on a load of washing so she'd have work clothes for the week ahead. Boris walked round the house, sniffing everything, then spread himself across the couch. 'I think I'll go to the supermarket,' I told Tina. I wanted to re-establish my presence by filling the house with food and drink that *I'd* chosen. 'Do we have any beer in the house?'

She wrinkled her nose. 'Neither of us drinks beer. Adam certainly didn't.' The way she said it implied that Adam was far too refined for anything so common.

'I'll buy some. It's what Charlotte drinks. And are you happy with lasagna for dinner?'

'Don't tell me; it's what Charlotte likes. What's her favorite color? Do we need to repaint the walls?'

Compared to the changes we'd made because Tina wanted Adam in our lives, buying beer and lasagna wasn't too much of an inconvenience. I didn't point this out, though. Tina and I were getting on better than I'd expected, given the circumstances. I didn't want to spoil it.

Boris saw me putting on my coat. Leaping from the couch, he sat between me and the front door. I think he was afraid I was going to disappear for another month. I promised him I'd only be gone half an hour. He grumbled, but stood aside to let me pass.

When I came home, Tina looked inside my shopping bag. 'I thought you were going to make your own,' she said, pulling out a pack of microwavable lasagna. 'A ready meal washed down with beer. Maybe this will be the year we achieve all our white trash goals.'

I spent the rest of the afternoon cleaning. I didn't think Charlotte would care about the state of our house but it's what I did while I was waiting for any guest to arrive. At seven o'clock, the doorbell rang. Opening the door, I found Charlotte, looking a little nervous, as if she wasn't sure how she'd be received. She was given a warm welcome by one member of the family. Boris leapt up at her as soon as she stepped into the hall. She was the perfect height for him to put his paws on her shoulders. She didn't shy away. Putting her arms around him, she ran her hands up and down his spine, making his tail wag even faster.

After he'd let her go, I gave her a hug and breathed in her scent—strong perfume with a hint of her sweat. She wasn't dressed up the way she'd been the night before, but she was a little smarter than she'd have been for an evening in her own room. She wore a gray, sleeveless crop-top with black trousers and heavy boots. Her face was made up in her trademark gothic style with black eyeshadow and heavy mascara. She followed me into the den.

Tina had changed out of the clothes from lost property. She was casually sexy in jeans and a blue sweater, which was deliberately an inch too short, showing off the skin above her waistband. Charlotte gave a hum of approval as she saw how good Tina looked. I wondered if they'd still be awkward with each other. But Charlotte took a bold approach. Putting her arms around Tina, she said, 'Sweetie, I know what we did yesterday wasn't your normal Saturday night. Maybe we'll do it again, maybe we won't. But, whatever happens, I want to be your friend.' It seemed to work. Tina visibly relaxed. She sat in the armchair and pointed Charlotte toward the couch.

'Do you want a beer, Charlotte?' I asked. She nodded. 'Tina?'

'I'll have my usual, babe.'

I went into the kitchen and took two cans of beer out of the fridge. I poured Tina a glass of the white wine Adam had left. When I went back into the den, Charlotte was talking about her job. 'Whatever shit the customers fling at me, I have to keep smiling. They reckon I'm personally responsible for putting toilet paper in their rooms and making sure their toast is gluten-free.'

I gave them their drinks and crouched on the floor with my beer, so I could rub Boris's belly.

'Don't take this the wrong way,' said Tina. 'But you don't seem the type to keep smiling. You look perfectly capable of telling people to fuck off.'

Charlotte laughed, showing her small, perfectly white teeth. 'You're right. I spent most of school and college telling my teachers just that. And maybe that's *why* I went into a service industry. I even thought of joining the Army.' Tina shook her head, uncomprehendingly. I was surprised, too. Charlotte was less than five feet tall and couldn't have weighed more than a hundred pounds. It was hard to imagine her as a soldier. 'It's what some born rebels do. Kicking against the system becomes so exhausting that we put ourselves in an environment where rebellion is impossible and there's nothing we can say except, "Yes, sir." I'm not saying the hotel's like the Army. The front office boss is no hard-bitten sergeant. But he knows I want to keep my job, so I'm not going to be rude to the guests. And he's happy for me to shout at him when I have to vent.' She laughed again and, looking more relaxed, stretched her arms above her head.

Tina drank half her wine in one go and said, 'My husband loves your armpits.'

'Does he?' said Charlotte, raising her eyebrows with feigned innocence. 'And what do *you* think of them?'

Tina sidestepped the question and asked, 'Why do you keep them like that?'

Charlotte leaned forward, the way she did when about to explain her views on life. 'Why shouldn't I? There are two things that happen to us when we hit puberty. We grow breasts ....' She placed her hands on her chest with a sorrowful look and said, 'Well, most of us do. And we get hairy. Why do people drool over the boobs but hate the hair? It's an appalling double standard. I have hair under my arms because I'm a woman, not a little girl.'

'I see what you mean.'

'But, if I remember … you don't agree.'

'I shaved my pits from the moment I spotted the first hairs,' said Tina. 'It wasn't to make myself more attractive or anything. I thought it's just what girls do. My pussy's more to do with being a cuckoldress. I asked Rob to shave it because I thought another guy would like it. And now I keep it this way as a message. When Rob sees it, he's reminded that the most intimate part of my body is always ready for someone else.'

Charlotte gave her a knowing look. 'So shaving is an act of low-level meanness.'

'A what?' asked Tina.

'It's a term I coined for the things Natalie used to do to me.'

'Who's Natalie?'

Charlotte spread her hands. 'Who indeed? She was my ….. It sounds strange to call her my girlfriend, because that sounds cute and romantic.' She took a mouthful of beer and reached over to tickle Boris's ear.

'You still miss her?' asked Tina.

Charlotte shook her head vigorously. 'No way. I hate her.' But her eyes were bloodshot.

Tina stood up and crossed to the couch. Sitting next to Charlotte, she said, 'Is it okay to hug you?'

'Don't worry. I won't turn into a nymphomaniac the moment you touch me.'

'That wouldn't necessarily be a bad thing,' said Tina. 'But for the moment, come here.'

Tina put her arms around Charlotte, who laid her head on Tina's breast. She looked so small in Tina's embrace and made Tina appear large and womanly by comparison. 'I'm okay,' said Charlotte. Tina gave her a final squeeze and went back to her chair. Charlotte took another swig from her bottle. 'Natalie would probably have called herself my domme or my mistress.'

'So what did that make you?'

'What do you think?' asked Charlotte, with a teasing smile.

'A masochist?' suggested Tina, tentatively.

I knew what Charlotte was going to say. 'We're all a mixture of sadism and masochism. But with Natalie, I normally played the submissive or bottom role.'

'It's not something I know much about,' said Tina.

'I'll take you to a BDSM club some time, if you like.'

Tina's eyes widened. 'Are there any round here?'

'Several,' said Charlotte. 'We had a favorite one, Pandora's Box. It's a little way out of town. We became features of the place—her leading me around on a leash, telling everyone she'd picked me up at the local pound.'

Tina looked thoughtful. 'I don't *think* I'd like that.' She paused and then added, 'But you never know.'

'Maybe you'd prefer some of her other acts of low-level meanness,' said Charlotte. 'She knew I liked to keep my pits hairy, so she told me they were gross and made me shave them. My body had to be the way *she* wanted it.' Tina gave a little moan. 'You like *that* idea,' said Charlotte. 'Do you want to make me change my body or do you want *me* to make *you*?'

Tina shook her head. 'I'm not sure.'

'Like I said, we're all a mixture. You don't have to choose.'

Tina sat forward. 'What else did she do to you?'

'A lot of my clothes bought it.'

Tina nodded enthusiastically. 'I like it when a guy's so desperate for me he can't wait to pull my panties down; he just rips a hole in them.'

'One time, Natalie told me to put on my favorite dress so she could burn holes in it with her cigarette.'

The growl of desire at the back of Tina's throat worried me. I didn't like to think how much we'd already spent on underwear that had been destroyed on its first outing. If this started happening to dresses, it would get very expensive very quickly.

'I can show you something else she used to do,' said Charlotte. 'Only if you want me to.'

Tina looked around the room, as if trying to work out what could happen, here in our den. Biting her lip, she said, 'Okay.'

'Give me your glass.'

Tina handed it over. Charlotte's cheeks moved slightly as she filled her mouth with saliva. She spat it all into Tina's wine and passed the glass back with the words, 'Drink it straight down, bitch.' Tina didn't hesitate. Lifting the glass to her lips, she drained it. Charlotte gave her an encouraging smile. 'Well done. How did that make you feel?'

Tina held her glass out to me and I refilled it. She was breathing heavily and her hand shook. Taking a sip of unadulterated wine to calm herself, she spoke slowly. 'Spitting in someone's drink is disgusting, but ….'

She trailed off and Charlotte finished the sentence. 'But you're horny as hell right now and you're not sure why.' She went back into teacher mode. 'Sex has this amazing power to transform bad into good. If I stub my toe when I'm getting out of bed in the morning, I don't have an orgasm. I swear like everyone else. But when Natalie gave my ass *serious pain*, it hurt more than a stubbed toe ever did, but I was in ecstasy, because it was sexy. It excited her to hurt me, and that excited me. Pain is bad, but sex makes it good.' Charlotte looked from Tina to me with an *Any questions?* expression. When neither of us said anything, she added, 'And it's the same with disgust. I'm guessing you suck Rob's dick.'

Tina gave me a playful look. 'I'd prefer not to, but sometimes duty calls.'

Charlotte smiled briefly, but didn't want to be distracted from her point. 'Rob's dick is disgusting.' She waved her hand at me. 'No offense, sweetie.'

A sexy woman insulting my cock was always more likely to turn me on than offend me, so I waved back at her. 'Don't worry.'

'It sits in his shorts sweating all day except when he takes it out and pisses through it. And you're putting it in your mouth?'

Tina shuddered slightly. 'When you say it like that ….'

'This isn't a dig at men,' said Charlotte. 'Eating pussy is just as bad, but sex makes disgusting things exciting.'

There was a silence while Charlotte let this sink in. It wasn't the best time to talk about food, but time was getting on. 'Are you hungry?' I asked Charlotte. 'We have lasagna.'

'Talking of disgusting things,' said Tina, grimly. 'Any way you can make *that* exciting?'

Charlotte ignored her and said, 'Sounds great.'

It took me a few minutes to put the lasagnas through the microwave. Going into the dining room, I saw Charlotte and Tina sitting next to each other at the table, chatting away happily. Tina was telling Charlotte anecdotes about David, her boss—stories I'd heard a hundred times before, but which were new to Charlotte.

Tina was so caught up in the conversation she forgot to be appalled by what she was eating and finished her lasagna. Pushing her plate away, she said, 'There's apple pie in the fridge.' She added wistfully, 'I made it for Adam …. Was it only yesterday?'

'A lot's happened since then,' I said. 'Do you want some pie?' I asked Charlotte, who responded with a yummy noise.

When we all had plates of pie with ice cream in front of us, Tina asked Charlotte, 'So, this whole domme … sub … sado masochist … whatever you call it. How long have you been into it?'

'Ever since I can remember,' said Charlotte. 'Lots of people play doctors and nurses when they're young. They use medical procedures as an excuse to show each other their sticky bits. But, for me, I always wanted it to be a punishment. I wasn't in hospital: I was in prison. I'd committed a crime so heinous I had to lie on a bed and have my genitals prodded.'

'It's not a sentence judges are allowed to hand down anymore,' I said.

'And when I discovered masturbation, I wasn't sure what

this strange new feeling was. I thought it was some kind of pain. I imagined myself being strapped to a machine that rubbed my clit until I couldn't take it anymore.'

'Where can I buy one of those?' asked Tina.

Charlotte took a sip of her beer, then put the can on the table, screwing up her face. 'Something wrong?' I asked her.

She put a hand to her throat. 'It's fine. It's … nothing.'

Tina was too much caught up in her fascination with this new world to notice. 'That club where Natalie used to take you …?'

'Pandora's Box.'

'What's it like?'

Charlotte shook herself slightly and considered the question. 'It costs a lot to get in, so most of the people who go there are doing all right. It's one of the few places where it doesn't pay to be a single heterosexual man.'

'But you said there's no such thing as—' I began.

'They don't know that,' said Charlotte. 'If a master goes in with his slave boy, there's no problem—so long as the "boy" is at least twenty-one. But if a guy on his own tries to get in just to perv on everyone else, he'll probably be turned away.' She stopped and rolled her eyes. 'And another thing: no one in BDSM agrees on anything—even what it stands for. Most people say it's bondage, discipline, sadism, and masochism. Others say the D is for domination and the S for submission. Some believe you can only be a *slave* if you have a contract with your master and live the lifestyle 24/7. If you only do it from time to time, you're a *submissive*. One person will tell you age play and CGL are essentially the same. Another will say they're completely different.' Tina looked overwhelmed by all these new terms she was hearing. Charlotte noticed and patted Tina's shoulder. 'Don't worry; it's like anything. If you play golf, you talk about sand wedges and unplayable lies. If you get into BDSM, you'll soon be talking about CBT, edgeplay, and all manner of good stuff.'

Tina took a drink and put her hands on the table in front

of her. 'Let's see if I understand this. If I like being spanked, it makes me a masochist.'

'It means you have certain masochistic tendencies,' said Charlotte.

Tina held up her hand, as if this was a subtlety she didn't want to get into. 'But I like people saying nasty things about my body. Does that mean I'm submissive?'

'No,' said Charlotte, 'enjoying humiliation is still masochistic. If you want to be told what to do, you're submissive.'

'So drinking your spit was masochistic.'

'But if you liked me *ordering* you to drink it, that was submissive.' Tina looked as if it was starting to make sense. 'But the most important thing about BDSM is there's no anger or malice in it.'

Remembering how angry I'd been when I spanked Tina, I shot her an apologetic glance. She saw it, but didn't look like she understood.

Charlotte continued, 'Even if you piss on someone and call them a piece of shit, you're really saying, "You turn me on—I want to turn you on, as well." But when the hurting is about rage or revenge, rather than sex, it's not BDSM anymore: it's abuse. If a master has too many beers on Friday night and gives his slave a black eye, he's no better than any other drunken asshole. Context is everything.' She looked away and I could see her eyes moistening again. 'It was where the trouble started with Natalie. She'd been screwed over by her last girlfriend and that made her angry at all women—well, all *people*. But I was the one in her bed so I was a convenient outlet. She hurt me in lots of ways because she was angry.'

'It must have been scary … but also exciting,' said Tina.

'It was,' admitted Charlotte. 'She was incredibly sexy—damn her.' Charlotte was sad for a moment, then looked at Tina and said, 'You seem very interested in this.'

Tina nodded. 'A few months ago, I'd have said it wasn't my thing, at all. But, as Rob says, a lot's happened since then.'

'Would you like to try something else?'

'Like what?'

'Rob,' said Charlotte, 'could you turn the heating up?'

'Are you cold?'

She shivered slightly, but said, 'That's not the reason.'

I went to the dial and turned it up. Tina had an exhilarated fear in her eyes, like someone stepping on to a roller coaster. Charlotte reassured her, 'You don't have anything to worry about. I'll know if it's too much for you. Some people use a safe word. The domme doesn't listen if the sub says, "That's enough," or "Please don't," but the moment she says, "Betelgeuse," or whatever the agreed word is, everything stops. Now, *I* don't think it should reach that point. If you care for someone, you should be able to read what's happening in her eyes. You know if she's still into it or if it's all gotten too much.' Charlotte paused and looked down, sadly. 'When Natalie saw the pleasure fade out of my eyes, leaving only the pain, it turned her on even more.' There was a silence. Then Charlotte looked up and smiled at Tina. 'I will know if you're all right. And if you're not, I *will* stop.'

'Okay,' said Tina. 'What do we do?'

'I need you to undress.' This seemed a good start to me and Tina's eyes sparkled, so she obviously liked the idea, as well. Staying in her chair, she pulled her sweater over her head. 'Look at you,' said Charlotte. 'I don't think I took the time last night to appreciate just how gorgeous you are.'

I agreed. I never wavered in my appreciation of Tina's looks. After experimenting with different styles, she had her dark brown hair once more spiked up into her trademark porcupine quills. Her intelligent eyes and strong nose gave her face character as well as beauty. As she reached behind her back to unhook her bra, Charlotte's eyes—and mine—were irresistibly drawn to Tina's natural 34C breasts.

Charlotte was trying to be the domme in this scene, but she looked shy as she asked, 'Is it okay if I ...?'

'Help yourself,' said Tina, pushing out her chest.

Charlotte's dominant position was further undermined

when she knelt at Tina's feet and reached up to massage Tina's breasts with her small hands. She was too short to suck Tina's nipple from there, so Tina bent forward. The sight of Tina feeding her pendulous left breast into Charlotte's mouth made my cock throb. Charlotte ran her tongue around Tina's nipple and bit it gently, making Tina moan. I could happily have watched this all night and was sad when Charlotte sat back on her heels and said, 'That was a detour. It's your fault for having such suckable tits.'

'Sorry,' said Tina, without looking it.

'Bottom half, as well.'

Tina stood up and pulled down her jeans and panties. Charlotte took a moment to gaze appreciatively. She may have had ideological issues with Tina's shaven cunt, but she couldn't deny it looked good.

Standing up, Charlotte put her hands on Tina's upper arms. 'You'll have to trust me,' said Charlotte. 'I wish I could say, "This won't hurt," but that would be a lie.'

Tina didn't resist as Charlotte gently pushed her toward the radiator. They stopped when Tina's butt was two inches away from the hot metal. 'Can you feel the heat?' asked Charlotte. Tina nodded. 'Imagine how it would feel if the sensitive skin of your ass touched it.'

Charlotte put her arms around Tina and leaned forward. Although Charlotte didn't weigh much, Tina rocked back, pressing the cheeks of her ass into the radiator. She sucked in air sharply as the pain hit her, but Charlotte didn't move, holding Tina firmly in position. After thirty seconds, Charlotte relaxed her grip.

Tina walked unsteadily back to the table. Her eyes were wide with her pupils dilated. She breathed heavily through her mouth. 'That was … *wrong*,' she said. From Tina, that was high praise.

'How did it feel?' asked Charlotte.

Tina sat down and gasped as her sore buttocks touched the chair. She took a sip of her drink and was quiet for a moment.

'It wasn't a tingling. That *hurt*. I didn't know if I could take it. But, at the same time, it was reassuring to be in your arms. You helped me get through the pain, even though you were the one causing it.'

'And that's the very heart of BDSM,' said Charlotte, looking at Tina like she was a student making good progress. Charlotte took Tina's hands in hers. 'This is another important thing,' said Charlotte. '*Aftercare*. When the excitement of a scene is over, there's a danger of *subdrop*. The sub feels guilty, ashamed, or plain sad about what's happened. Usually, it's nothing more than a bad case of post-orgasmic blues, but it *can* hit you like the flu. So it's important to make sure the sub is okay. Apply some cooling lotion to the parts that are hurting. Give a bit of reassurance: "You may be a sub, but you're still important to me. Even if I hurt you, I'll always look after you." As you can imagine, Natalie wasn't big on aftercare.'

'Maybe you'd feel better if you didn't talk about her so much,' I suggested, gently.

Charlotte didn't pay any attention. 'There's also *domdrop*. The dominant sometimes feels guilty about what they've done and crashes once the scene's over. Natalie was always fine.' She continued before I could make any further attempt to stop her obsessing. 'What were you focused on while we were doing that?' she asked Tina.

Tina gave her a look, as if that was a silly question. 'Er … the searing pain in my butt.'

'Were you thinking about your job, the economy, climate change?'

'Not at all,' said Tina.

'Exactly. You were totally in the moment. Masochists were the original mindfulness practitioners.'

It seemed Tina wasn't ready to become totally submissive yet. Opening her legs, she pointed at the floor in front of her. Charlotte knelt down again and looked up at Tina innocently. 'Anything you want?'

Grabbing two handfuls of crow-black hair, Tina pulled

Charlotte's face into her crotch. 'Look what you've done to me,' said Tina.

Charlotte dipped her tongue into Tina's cunt. Moving her head back a little, she said, 'I appear to have made you very wet.'

Charlotte used her fingers to part Tina's labia. The tip of Charlotte's tongue flickered against the end of Tina's clit—teasing her with as little contact as possible. Tina seemed to enjoy the delicious frustration for a while, but then put her hands behind Charlotte's head and pulled her closer. Charlotte licked along Tina's inner lips. Tina closed her eyes and groaned softly as Charlotte applied her expert tongue.

I didn't feel any jealousy as I watched Charlotte pleasuring my wife. It was different than seeing her with another man. *That* was watching someone else doing what I should have been doing. *My wife wouldn't have to do this if I were a better man.* I didn't feel Charlotte was taking my place. I'd licked Tina's cunt hundreds of times, but I could never be a *woman* licking it. Charlotte knew how it felt to have her cunt licked well and so knew exactly what to do. Tina was soon gripping the seat of her chair as she threw her head back in ecstasy. It took only a couple of minutes until I saw the signs she was close to cumming. Charlotte must have picked up on these too, because she broke off from what she was doing to look up at Tina and say, 'I can show you another mean thing Natalie used to do to me. I can ruin your orgasm.'

For a moment, Tina looked intrigued, but, pushing Charlotte's face back into her cunt, she said, 'Don't ruin anything. Give me the best fucking orgasm you've got.'

Charlotte focused again on Tina's clit. This time, there was no teasing. Charlotte used the flat of her tongue to lick Tina, fast and urgently. Tina stroked her own breasts. Twisting her nipples hard, she came with a shout. Grinning contentedly, she slumped in her chair. As the sensations subsided, she sat up straighter. 'Do I do you, now?' she asked, uncertainly, as if unfamiliar with the etiquette of girl-on-girl sex.

Charlotte shook her head. 'Actually, sweetie, it's been a long day. All of a sudden, I'm beat. I'd better get back to the hotel.'

'Why don't you stay here?' suggested Tina. 'Rob can run you back in the morning.'

It was nice of Tina to volunteer me, but I liked the idea of Charlotte staying over. Charlotte agreed immediately: she looked like she wanted to go to bed as soon as possible. Tina picked up her clothes and we all went upstairs. Boris followed, but stayed on the landing. Experience had taught him that, when there were three people in the bed, there was no room for him. 'Do you want anything to wear in bed?' Tina asked Charlotte.

Charlotte shook her head. 'I don't think I have much you guys haven't already seen.' She took off all her clothes.

'If it's good enough for you …' said Tina, and put the pile of clothes she was carrying on the chair.

With the ladies taking this free and easy attitude to nudity, I couldn't insist on flannel pajamas, so I started undressing.

Charlotte's body was still new to me. Her pale skin was punctuated by tattoos—some professional, others crudely drawn—and by thick bushes of dark hair under each arm and around her cunt. She'd eaten all her lasagna and apple pie, but still looked like she hadn't eaten in a week. Her breasts were mere nodules with large red-brown nipples. I would never have said someone like her was *my type*. But my cock was at full size just from being in the same room with her. I made sure I was gazing lustfully at Tina as I took off my shorts. It was the first time Charlotte had seen my cock. She raised her eyebrows and said, 'Not a regular cuckold, are you, Rob?'

Tina had to chime in with, 'Rob's dick is like a rhinoceros—surprisingly quick for its size.'

I hoped one of them would say, 'There's an erect penis in the room—shouldn't we do something about it?' But they got into bed without giving it another thought.

Tina seemed more comfortable with Charlotte and held her tight. I put my arm around both of them and we went to sleep.

Chapter Three

~

I WAS GETTING USED TO waking up with two naked women in my bed. It would have been great to spend the day watching Tina and Charlotte together. Unfortunately, it was Monday morning and real life intruded. I got out of bed, threw on the first clothes I could find, and went onto the landing, where Boris was already limbering up. I took him out and we ran twice around the park. Letting myself back into the house, I found Tina in her bathrobe, waiting for me. 'Charlotte's hot,' she said.

Something in her expression made me worried, but I tried for a joke. 'You've only just noticed?'

'I'm serious, Rob.'

'Is she sick?'

'I think so. She's still asleep, but she's sweating a lot.' I told my cock sternly this was *not* the time to be aroused by the thought of Charlotte sweating.

Tina rummaged through the kitchen cupboards until she found the thermometer and we went upstairs. Charlotte had gravitated to the middle of the empty bed. I sat next to her and put my hand on her arm. Opening her eyes, she managed a half-smile as she croaked, 'Hey, Rob.'

'How are you feeling?' I asked.

She paused as if she had to think about this before saying, 'Not great, if I'm honest.' She put her hand to her throat. 'There are some types of pain that definitely don't turn me on.'

'Is it okay if I take your temperature?' I asked.

'Anywhere you like,' she said.

I was tempted, but settled for slipping the thermometer into her mouth. After five minutes, I took it out, looked at it, and passed it to Tina.

Tina read it and silently mouthed, 'Fuck!' at me.

'You're burning up,' I told Charlotte.

She managed to lift herself into a half-sitting position. 'Probably a virus. I'll go back to the hotel and sleep it off.'

'You're not going anywhere, honey,' said Tina.

'But I can't—' began Charlotte.

'Yes, you can,' said Tina. 'You stay here until you're ready to be released back into the wild.' She turned to me, her voice more businesslike. 'I've got my laptop, so I can work from home this morning. But there's a meeting this afternoon I can't miss.'

'I've only one lesson this afternoon,' I said. 'But I can ask Gareth to do it. I covered for him when he was hungover last week, so he owes me.'

Charlotte pushed the quilt away and tried to get out of bed. 'I'm fine,' she said. 'You don't have to—'

'Didn't you order bed rest for this patient, doctor?' Tina asked me.

'Indeed I did, nurse,' I replied.

'Why do you assume I'm the nurse, you sexist bastard? I could just as easily be the attending physician.'

'My bad,' I said, gently pushing Charlotte back into bed.

I tucked the quilt around her, but she was still shivering. I went to fetch the spare quilt I used when I was banished to the couch. After Charlotte was bundled up in both of them, she went back to sleep.

Gareth was happy to cover my two o'clock lesson, so I

arrived back from the language school a little after one. Tina was on the couch, working at her computer and fanning herself. 'How's the patient?' I asked.

'She's had a slice of toast and some tea, but ….' She shook her head anxiously. 'I got dressed right in front of her and she didn't even look.'

'She *must* be sick. I could be at death's door and I'd still check out your ass.'

'And she was still complaining of the cold, so I've turned up the heating.' She put her laptop on the arm of the couch and stood up. 'Let's see how she's doing, then I have to go.'

'By the way, where's Boris?' I asked. He usually ran to meet me when I came home.

'He was around,' said Tina. 'I haven't seen him in a while.'

We went upstairs and both stopped short as we reached the bedroom door. Charlotte was still in the middle of the bed with Boris snuggled up beside her, keeping her warm. She had her arm around his chest, holding him like a giant teddy bear. They were both asleep. Tina and I spent a few moments in the doorway watching them, before stealing away.

Tina went off to work. I sat in the den and marked assignments for two hours. Then I crept upstairs and looked in. Charlotte and Boris both raised their heads as I opened the door. 'Hi, sweetie,' said Charlotte, in a throaty rasp.

'You feeling any better?' I asked, sitting on the bed and tickling Boris behind his ear.

She made a face. 'Not really. There are times when I love spending all day in bed. This isn't one of them.'

'Do you want anything?'

'I could do with a beer.'

'I'm not sure your doctor would like that.'

'So don't give one to my doctor.'

I went downstairs and got a couple of beers out of the fridge. I picked up my laptop before going back to the bedroom. I sat on the bed with my back against the headboard and opened the laptop. Charlotte put her head on my shoulder so she could see the screen and sip her beer. Her body was pressed against mine. She'd been lying in bed all day, sweating profusely. Some would have said she needed to shower and douse herself with deodorant. But to me, her natural scent was beautiful and sexy. I had to tell myself again this wasn't the time to be turned on. I knew the two types of movie Charlotte liked and asked her, '*Sleepless in Seattle* or *Driller Killer*?'

'I don't think I can focus on a film,' she said. 'Can we watch some things on YouTube?'

We watched a variety of clips. We saw incontrovertible proof that Paul McCartney is dead while Jim Morrison's still alive. We heard it's ridiculous to think a man has ever walked on the moon, but perfectly reasonable to believe the world is ruled by alien lizards. We also watched reviews of films we'd never seen.

To start with, Charlotte kept up a flow of amusingly sour comments. After an hour, though, she went quiet and I heard a soft snore. Taking the can out of her hand, I placed it on the bedside table. Her head was still on my shoulder, so I couldn't move without disturbing her. I watched a couple more clips, but I think I must have fallen asleep, as well. The next thing I knew, Boris's tail was slapping my leg showing he was happy about something. I heard a key in the lock followed by footsteps coming up the stairs. Tina came into the room. A normal wife would have hit the ceiling on finding her husband in bed with a naked woman, but our marriage had stopped being normal a long time ago and Tina barely raised an eyebrow. I thought maybe she looked sad for a second, but smiled when Boris rolled onto his back for her. Rubbing his belly, Tina asked, 'How's she doing?'

I pointed to the can of beer. 'She's more like herself.'

'Good. Are you watching lesbian porn?'

'I wish. It's stuff on YouTube.'

'Can I join you?'

'If Boris doesn't mind.'

'Do you want another drink?'

'Why not? It doesn't look like being an evening of high achievement.' Tina went downstairs. I was surprised when she came back a minute later with two cans of beer. 'You hate beer,' I reminded her.

'I thought I'd give it another chance,' she replied.

She sat on the bed and pressed herself tightly against me. Taking a sip of beer, she shuddered. 'People like this stuff?' she said, incredulously. 'It's like drinking pee.' She added hastily, 'Well, I should imagine it is.'

'If that's something you want to try, I'm sure Charlotte will oblige.'

We watched a couple of clips, but Tina didn't get into them, and I'd been sitting in the same place for long enough. Charlotte opened her eyes for a second as I moved my shoulder from under her, but when I laid her head on the pillow, she went back to sleep.

Tina and I went downstairs and made dinner. We ate in our "normal" way—next to each other on the couch, watching a crime drama on TV. The only problem was it didn't feel normal anymore. It felt more normal for Tina to share the couch with another man, after she'd pointedly relegated me to the chair. It felt more normal to eat at the table with other people, discussing topics that could be exciting and soul-crushing, often at the same time. But Tina and I did our best to pretend. We even used our catchphrase, 'I do not have high hopes for his future,' when we saw someone on the screen in danger.

At nine o'clock, we heard movement from the bedroom and went to check on Charlotte. She was awake and wanted to get up for a while, so she came downstairs and we fed her chicken noodle soup.

We were all back in bed before ten.

When the alarm went off on Tuesday morning, Charlotte said she was feeling a little better. She wasn't ready to go back to the hotel, but Tina and I decided she could be left in Boris's care. When we arrived home in the evening, Charlotte declared herself well enough to go out for a while, so the four of us took a walk.

But we knew Charlotte was really herself again on Wednesday evening. We were sitting round the table. Charlotte was wearing a pair of Tina's pajamas. They were too long for her, so she had to keep pulling up the sleeves. She'd eaten a hearty dinner, and drunk a couple of beers. 'How are you feeling now?' Tina asked her.

Charlotte looked at her and grinned. 'Horny.'

Tina laughed. 'That's my girl.' Then she asked, 'Do you want to do anything about it?'

Charlotte spread her hands. 'Your house. Your rules.'

Tina blushed and took a sip of her wine. 'Well, there is one thing I've been thinking ….'

'Share with the group,' said Charlotte.

'Well … I was wondering if you could … be mean to me again. Only if you're well enough, of course.'

'What are you thinking of now?' asked Charlotte.

Tina looked shy again. 'You mentioned something Natalie used to do … you know … to your dresses.'

'I get you,' said Charlotte. 'Did I see a pack of cigarettes lying around somewhere?'

Tina nodded. 'Emma left them here. I've told her, but she hasn't bothered to pick them up. Ben makes sure she always has hundreds at home.'

'Then she won't mind if I steal a couple.'

'She won't even notice.'

'Well, why don't you go and put on a pretty dress? Maybe not your latest Gucci, but ….' She paused and gave her own version of the wicked look. '… it should be one that means something.'

Tina went upstairs. She was gone a long time and I heard the sound of her moving a chair across the floor, like she was looking for something to stand on. All her dresses were in an easily accessible wardrobe, so I wondered what she was doing.

Charlotte looked at me. 'Are you okay with this, Rob?'

'Oh yes,' I said. 'The ability to hold two opposite ideas at the same time is supposed to be a sign of intelligence. It's also a sign of being a cuckold. In a way, I hate what's about to happen. But … if you don't do it, I'll spend the rest of my life regretting I never got to see it.'

'Remember what I said about the eyes. If I look into *yours* and see it's all too much, that'll stop everything, as well.' We sat in silence for a moment, before she asked, 'Which one do you think she'll pick?'

'It's not like she has hundreds to choose from. I reckon she'll go with the scarlet silk one. She wore it when we faced down her first lover, so maybe she'll wear it to show she can't face down a strong woman.'

As Tina descended the stairs, I heard the swish of fabric against the walls. She didn't usually wear billowing dresses, so I couldn't picture which one it was. She stood in the doorway and looked at us with a mischievous defiance. 'How do I look?' she asked.

My mouth fell open, as did Charlotte's. 'Oh, sweetie, are you sure?' Charlotte asked, in a whisper.

'Quite sure,' said Tina, but looked at me as if she thought— or maybe hoped—this was one of those moments when I'd step in to stop things.

She was wearing her wedding dress. I was shocked to see her in it. She hadn't worn it since the day of our marriage. It had been folded in a box on top of the wardrobe. It was an ankle-length dress in ivory tulle. The skirt was lace with an opaque underskirt. The shoulder straps broadened out to form a split floral pattern bodice. As on our wedding day, she wasn't wearing anything under it. There was a promise that, in the right light, her nipples would be visible through the fabric. I'd spent our wedding day trying to catch a glimpse. Probably some of our guests had, as well. It was a little snugger around the hips than the first time she'd worn it, but she still looked great.

She handed Charlotte the open pack of Yves Saint Laurent

cigarettes and the expensive S.T. Dupont lighter which Emma had casually forgotten. Charlotte took out a cigarette, but stopped as she was raising it to her lips and looked from me to Tina. 'Is it okay to smoke in the house?' Even when being a dominatrix, she didn't forget her manners. We both nodded and Charlotte lit the cigarette. She wasn't used to it and squinted to avoid the smoke. The narrowing of her eyes gave her a cruel look. I realized how heavily I was breathing and tried to control it. Charlotte moved her chair to sit opposite Tina. Taking a drag on the cigarette, she pointed the glowing end at the dress.

'Please don't,' said Tina.

Charlotte looked up. Seeing Tina's eyes still shining with lust, she said, 'Shut up, bitch.'

Charlotte pulled the fabric away from Tina's right breast and pressed the cigarette against it. She sat back to admire the damage. The hole in the dress was bigger than I'd expected— the size of a penny. The hole's border was black with an outer ring of dirty brown. Charlotte took another drag and pressed the cigarette onto the skirt of the dress between Tina's legs. She took care not to burn Tina's skin. I guessed that was a different game. She looked around for an ashtray, but we hadn't thought of that, so I gave her my empty dessert bowl. She flicked her ash into it and went back to the dress, applying the burning tip to the front of it. I thought she might spell out "BITCH" or "WHORE" in holes, but there was no pattern. By the time the cigarette had burned down to the filter, Tina's dress looked like it had been blasted with buckshot.

Charlotte stubbed out the cigarette in my bowl. 'Another?' she asked Tina.

'No, that's enough,' said Tina.

Charlotte looked into Tina's eyes and realized Tina meant it. We sat quietly for a while. Even though none of us had cum, it felt like post-orgasmic sadness. It reminded me of what one of my colleagues had said about the one and only time he went on a pheasant shoot. After the excitement was over, he wanted the birds to stand up and fly away. And now, part of me wanted Tina's wedding dress to be back the way it was. But, on the whole, I was glad I hadn't stopped them. Most people would say the dress had been destroyed, but, for me, it still had a certain beauty. The black and brown marks reminded me of a leopard's spots. And I felt, perversely, that the dress was now a better symbol of our marriage—hanging together despite the damage.

After Tina had said, 'That's enough,' I thought we'd pretend nothing had happened and go to bed or watch TV. So I was surprised when Tina asked, 'Did you say Natalie used to *ruin* your orgasms.'

'All the time,' said Charlotte, with a look both sad and nostalgic. 'She had me on the bed, naked, with my wrists and ankles tied to the bedposts.' My cock stiffened at this image. 'Then she licked or fingered me until I was nearly there.' I leaned forward so the bulge in my trousers wasn't too obvious. 'She knew my body so well she could tell the exact moment before I came. And that's when she'd pour a glass of cold water over my cunt. It left me so frustrated. If she felt particularly heartless—and she normally did—she took me to the point and then denied me five or six times. Then she'd walk away and there was nothing I could do except struggle impotently. I couldn't free my hands to touch myself. And she always tied my legs so they were *just* too far apart for me to squeeze my cunt between my thighs.' Obviously liking this image as much as I did, Tina moaned softly. 'Do you want me to give you a ruined orgasm?' asked Charlotte. Tina shook her head. 'Or do you want to give *me* one?'

Tina looked at me. 'I was wondering if it would work on a man.'

'I've never tried it on a guy,' said Charlotte. 'But I've seen it done at Pandora's Box loads of times. A man's strapped to the bench while his mistress gives him a ruined or a blocked.'

Tina threw up her hands. 'It's easier to learn Japanese than BDSM speak. What's the difference between a ruined and a blocked?'

'I could … demonstrate, if you like.'

'What do you say, babe?' Tina asked me.

I tried to keep my breathing calm, but I was sure they could both hear my heart pounding. I thought there was a real possibility Charlotte was about to touch my cock for the first time. I didn't want Tina to see how excited I was by this prospect, so I said casually, 'Whatever you want.'

'Okay,' said Charlotte. 'Could you get out … little Rob?' I stood up and pulled down my trousers and shorts. Sitting back down, I moved my shirt away from my hard cock. 'Right,' she said to Tina, 'kneel between your husband's legs.' I felt a momentary disappointment that Tina, rather than Charlotte, was going to touch me. But I quickly reminded myself that Tina's touch was pretty darn good. 'You'll have to work with us, Rob,' said Charlotte. 'I'm sure Tina knows your responses pretty well, and can tell when you're about to cum.'

'Oh yes,' said Tina, curling her lip, 'if his cock is anywhere near me, I know he's about to cum.'

Charlotte ignored the slight and told me, 'But in case she doesn't notice, it's important you let us know if you're on the verge. Don't cum without telling us.'

'Okay,' I said.

'Do you think we can trust him?' Charlotte asked Tina.

Tina responded by looking at me sternly and saying, 'If we can't, there's a tube of toothpaste with his name on it.'

'Now take hold of his dick and jerk him the way you normally do,' said Charlotte. Tina moved her hand up and down on my cock. 'When he's about to cum, put your thumb and pointing finger around the join where the head meets the shaft and squeeze as hard as you can.'

I wanted to hold on for as long as possible—partly to impress Charlotte, and also to show Tina that she was wrong about me. But I had a nasty feeling I was going to prove her right. I tried doing my tax return in my head, but getting a hand job from my wife while a sexy young goth gave her instructions was too much for me. I lasted less than a minute before shouting, 'I'm going to cum!' in a voice more high-pitched than I'd have liked.

Tina squeezed as hard as she could. I was momentarily stunned by the pain, like my brain couldn't process it. Tina didn't relax her grip so the pain didn't ease off. Dark purple spots of broken capillaries spread over my cock head. Added to the pain was the pressure building in my groin. Millions of sperm were desperate to escape, but there was nowhere for them to go. The pressure increased until I was afraid one of my balls would burst, but then gradually it subsided. But the crushing force around my cock remained until Tina was sure I was past the point of cumming and she let me go.

'How do you feel, Rob?' asked Charlotte.

'You know when your genitals have been run over by a truck?'

'It's never happened to me,' said Tina. 'But I can imagine.'

'They're still hurting now. It's worse than being kicked in the balls.' I held a cold can of beer against my cock and the pain slowly wore off.

'So that was a blocked one?' Tina asked Charlotte.

'Correct. We'll wait a few minutes, then try for a ruined. Okay with you, Rob?'

'Fine,' I said. I may have been in great pain, but two beautiful women were paying a lot of attention to my cock. That didn't happen every day, and I didn't want it to stop.

'Steve loved controlling my orgasms,' said Tina. 'He dictated when and if I had one. And *he* only came when he wanted to.' She gave me a withering look and said, 'Not at all what I was used to.'

'Blocked orgasms can also be used to treat premature …' began Charlotte. Then she gave me a guilty look. 'Sorry, Rob, this is none of my business.'

'Honey,' said Tina, 'my husband's showing you his cock. You're already pretty deep in our business.'

'Well, if Rob looks like cumming before you want him to,

you can block him, wait a few minutes, and he should be good to go again. Keep squeezing and he'll fuck you all night.'

'That would be a first.'

'Are you ready for round two?' Charlotte asked me.

Tina was ready. She knelt between my knees again and looked up at Charlotte—the good student waiting for her next lesson. 'Keep jerking him the way you were before. And, Rob, this time it's even more important you let us know when you're about to cum.'

I gave a little cry as Tina took hold of my sore cock. She heard this and pulled harder. The pain made my cock even more sensitive and I still had a lot of sperm anxious to leave my body, so I wasn't surprised when I felt myself cumming immediately. I was so desperate for release that I thought of saying nothing and risking the consequences. There was even part of me that wanted to see how Charlotte would react to me being punished. But I played the game and shouted, 'Now!'

'Pull your hands away, Tina!' said Charlotte. Tina instantly raised her hands as if in surrender. My cock pulsed but wasn't stimulated in any way. The sperm would not be denied again. It wasn't an ejaculation so much as a stream of semen oozing out of me, covering my balls and thighs. I couldn't speak for a moment. I had the same cold, prickly feeling as a teenager waking up from a wet dream. There was no pleasure or satisfaction. All I knew was that I had sperm all over me. 'You should feel more frustrated than if you hadn't cum.'

'I do,' I assured them.

'Now, we could tie his hands behind his back,' said Charlotte. 'Or we could trust him.'

'You're honor bound not to touch yourself tonight,' said Tina. 'Now, go and get cleaned up. And if you get any cum on the bathroom carpet, the toothpaste won't be on your balls: I'll squirt the whole tube up your ass.'

Before I went, I had to ask, 'What exactly do you want here, Tina? I thought we were talking about *you* being submissive. But a whole load of shit's landed on me.'

Tina looked me in the eye and said, 'Rob, I'm going to find a guy with a big, hard cock who knows what he's doing in bed. I'm going to let him hurt my body and mess with my mind. After that, I might have a certain amount of pent-up aggression, which I'm going to take out on you. Any questions?'

'No, it all seems pretty clear.'

She stood up and kissed the top of my head. 'Welcome to the bottom of the food chain, babe. Now, go and wipe yourself.'

I went into the bathroom, shutting the door behind me. Neither of them could see me and there was nothing to stop me from jerking off. But I didn't want to: it would have been a betrayal of Charlotte, Tina, and the game we were playing. Just then, it felt sexier *not* to cum.

Chapter Four

~

THE NEXT MORNING, I dropped Charlotte off at the hotel on my way to work. I was sad to see her go, but, arriving at the language school, I found Gareth had taken revenge by going off sick. I had to cover his lessons, which kept me too busy all day to think of anything else.

I felt down when I arrived home. I couldn't help thinking the evening would be more exciting with Charlotte there. We'd eat in the dining room and who knows where the conversation would go? Possibly to something painful or humiliating for me, but it wouldn't be boring. As it was, Tina and I were both tired and decided to have an early night. The bed seemed too big for two of us, and Boris wasted no time in hopping up and filling the empty space.

After two more evenings like this, Tina said, 'Babe, we *are* still allowed to have sex—you know, just the two of us.'

'It's a radical idea,' I said, joking to cover up my nervousness. Tina and I had been together seventeen years. We'd had sex hundreds, maybe thousands, of times. It should have been the easiest thing in the world to go upstairs and make love. But I was faced with the problem that had worried me continually over the past couple of months: I wasn't sure what the rules were.

Our standard hot wife and cuckold sex involved her comparing me unfavorably to another guy. Then I licked her until she came. If she let me fuck her, I was always so turned on that I came immediately, giving her the perfect opportunity to tease me some more. Then, with the game over, we curled up together and went to sleep like any other loving couple.

But I didn't know if we could still do that. The last man she'd been with was Adam. Given the rift he'd created between Tina and me, I didn't think we could use him in our fantasies.

Fortunately, once we were in the bedroom, Tina took control. 'Strip,' she said. I took my clothes off, while she did the same. 'Leave the light on.' She sometimes had me turn the light off, so it was easier for her to pretend I was someone else. But that wasn't what she had in mind here. We got into bed and she kissed me passionately. Then she asked, 'Do you wish Charlotte was here?'

I had to make a quick choice. Did Tina want me to desire another woman or not? Her mischievous look decided for me. 'Yes, I do,' I said.

'She's prettier than me. Prettier and sexier, and those tattoos make her look so slutty. You love sluts, don't you, babe?' I had a momentary pang of conscience. Should we be talking this way about our friend? 'But unfortunately,' Tina continued in a commiserating voice, 'she's into women. So you'll never have her.' That wasn't what Charlotte believed about herself, but I wasn't going to let mere facts ruin the sexy talk. 'All you can do is watch her licking my pussy and giving me the best cum of my life.' With no offense to Charlotte and her nimble tongue, I was fairly sure Tina's best cum had been with some bull's cock inside her, but, again, it wasn't the time to say anything. 'I know what you like best about Charlotte,' said Tina, putting her hands behind her head and showing me her armpits. Each had a thin covering of short, sharp hairs. 'What do you think, babe?' asked Tina. 'Your dream come true. A woman with hairy armpits who also loves cock.' Her armpits weren't as good as Charlotte's, but Charlotte had given hers years to grow and develop. Tina had only had a couple of days. Somehow, hairy armpits didn't look quite right on Tina. It was like a hat which looks great on one person, but doesn't suit another. Even so, I was grateful to her. For the last few months, she'd kept her body the way another man liked it. Now she was deliberately trying to be attractive to *me*. I wasn't going to let on that I was anything except ecstatic about this new development. I made an exaggerated noise of desire as I lay on top of her, kissing each armpit in turn. I must admit they did the job they were supposed to do. My cock was soon hard. I rolled a condom over it and entered her. As soon as I was inside, she said, 'You know it's only temporary, babe. As soon as I find me another hot stud, I'm going to shave them. Or rather, *you're* going to shave them. Watching you destroy something *you* love so I can get what *I* love. It would be the biggest turn-on ....'

She trailed off and looked at me with a strange mixture of triumph and resignation as she felt me cumming into the condom.

WE'D ARRANGED TO MEET Charlotte again on Thursday evening. Tina had booked us into The Bombardier, a new gastropub in town. The walls, floor, and ceiling were all pine, which made the main room look more like a sauna than a restaurant. The clean smell of fresh-cut wood hadn't yet been masked by kitchen aromas. When we arrived, Charlotte was already sitting at a table in the corner. It was testament to Tina's persuasive skills that Charlotte was out. She generally preferred to spend the evening in her room at the hotel. She looked great in a black and red sleeveless dress and a black bead necklace. As we walked toward her, I wondered if she was there as my friend or as Tina's ... lover? ... mentor? ... experiment? I told myself to stop over-thinking. I knew what Charlotte herself would say: *You're Rob, she's Tina, I'm Charlotte—why do we need any other labels?*

As if to show she was there for us both equally, she stepped out from behind the table and put her arms around our necks, pulling our faces down to hers. She kissed both of us on the lips, then released us so we could sit and look over the menu. The bar snacks were more appealing than the main dishes, so we asked the waiter to bring all six and put them in the middle of the table. Tina saw Gewürztraminer on the wine list and insisted we order that. It was one of her favorites since Adam had introduced us to it. Charlotte shrugged as if it wouldn't kill her to drink wine this one time.

We chatted about work. Charlotte had dealt with a hotel guest who thought there was a rat in his room and nothing would convince him there wasn't. Eventually, Charlotte had gone up to his room with a bag and come out a moment later, proudly announcing she'd caught the rat and was going to keep it as her familiar. The man had thought that was a perfectly reasonable thing for a goth girl to do and he'd gone to sleep.

Tina took a gulp of her wine and turned to Charlotte. 'The club you used to go to with Natalie … Pandora's Box.' I thought I spotted a fleeting annoyance in Charlotte's eyes, as if she was getting tired of this topic, but she nodded. 'If you … took us there, do you think we'd be okay?'

It was the first I'd heard of this idea.

'You'd probably get out alive,' replied Charlotte. Tina didn't laugh, so Charlotte asked, 'Why? Do you think it's the sort of place you'd like to go?'

'I'm not sure,' said Tina, quietly. 'Sometimes, I just want to stay at home and have fun with you.'

Charlotte put her hand on Tina's arm. 'Nothing wrong with that, sweetie.'

'You've opened so many doors in a couple of evenings. I'm sure there's much more I could learn from you.'

Charlotte grinned. 'I can think of a few more things we could try.'

'And … the thought of stepping through the door into a BDSM club ….'

'The door doesn't slam behind you,' said Charlotte. 'You

can always step out again if you don't like it. And a BDSM club isn't the Wild West. There are rules and people who make sure everyone sticks to them. Consent is crucial. If anyone came up to you and started a scene without asking, he'd be out the door in a second.'

'Even so …' said Tina.

'How does this sound?' said Charlotte. 'I take you there as my slave. If anyone asks if they can punish you, I'll say no, because you'd enjoy it too much. Unless, of course, you decide you want to be punished, in which case we'll have a signal and I'll let you go.'

'That could work,' said Tina. 'What would I wear?'

'Nothing too elaborate. A simple black dress with a collar to show you're taken.'

'And what about me?' I asked.

Charlotte turned to me. 'That all depends who you want to be. If you're my other slave, we can put you in a thong with a harness round your chest. If, however, you want to go as a dom, maybe a short leather coat over black trousers. But, on some club nights, there's a special concession for men who'd prefer not to adopt a particular role. They're allowed to wear black tie.' That sounded better than being paraded around in a thong. And now I had a tuxedo, I might as well use it.

My thoughts were interrupted by something familiar in my peripheral vision. Instinctively, I turned to look more closely. At the other side of the room was a long table where a group of eight men were sitting. There were twenty empty bottles on the table. I recognized one of the men. I lowered my head and hoped he wouldn't notice us. It didn't work. He stood up and came over to our table. The beer bottle in his hand obviously wasn't his first. There was a combative look in his eyes I hadn't seen before. 'Well, look who's here,' he said, with a slight slur in his voice.

Tina's surprise soon turned to anger. 'We're not talking to you, Nathan.'

Interpreting this as an invitation to join us, he sat down.

'What's wrong? We've always been friends.'

'Louise is my friend,' replied Tina, caustically. 'I tolerated you as part of the package.' This wasn't true. She'd always gotten on well with both of them.

Nathan looked at Charlotte with a leer that made me want to punch him. 'And who's this beauty?'

Charlotte met his eye unflinchingly and responded with a dead-pan, 'I'm their karate teacher. I've been showing them how to destroy a man's balls with a single kick.'

He didn't react and turned back to Tina. 'Why are you mad at me?'

'Louise told us what you've been doing.'

He laughed. 'I bet she did.'

Tina's tone changed from anger to disgust. 'How could you do it, Nathan? Louise worshipped you.'

'Did she? Tina, did you ever think maybe you've only heard one side of the story?'

Tina went back to being angry. 'Oh, it's *her* fault, is it? She doesn't understand you, I suppose.'

Nathan sighed and his face became serious, even sad. 'It wasn't that she didn't understand me. It was more she didn't need me.' He took a swig from his bottle. 'Like, whenever something happened to her, I was lucky if I made the top ten of people she told. She'd normally told her parents, her brother, and several of her friends before she got around to telling me. One time, when her car broke down in the middle of nowhere, she called her brother to pick her up. It's not like I was busy or anything. I was home watching TV and she knew that. So why didn't she call *me*? Then there was one time, I came home to find her dad fiddling around with my front door. Her key was stuck in the lock, and—of course—she called him. Now, you might think something like that shouldn't matter. And if it had only been a couple of times, I wouldn't have cared. But it happened again and again. Hundreds of little incidents like that wear you down.'

He paused and looked at us, as if trying to gauge whether

we understood what he was saying. I certainly did. When Tina had told Adam about her promotion at work before she'd told me, it had been much worse than watching her in bed with another guy. It was one thing for her to enjoy someone else's body. It was another to make him her confidant over me. I didn't particularly want to sympathize with Nathan, but I could see why he was so hurt by the feeling he wasn't Louise's go-to-guy. Tina was still looking mad. Some people would have been surprised at her reaction—surely she was the last person who should condemn someone for being unfaithful. But Tina was a cuckoldress, not a cheater. There was an important difference. She and I had discussed the idea of her having sex with other men before she did it. My lack of staying power in the bedroom had caused an issue between us, so we'd talked about it and come up with an idea. It was different than one of us going off independently to find a solution in someone else's bed. That Tina was thinking along the same lines was borne out by her next questions. 'Did it ever occur to you to talk to her about it? Tell her how you felt? Or do real men not do that sort of thing?'

Nathan snorted. 'Or maybe real women don't want to *hear* that sort of thing. Sure, I tried telling her, "Maybe when you have a problem, you could come to me." What was her reply? "Why are you trying to drive a wedge between me and my family? Do you want to stop me from seeing them?" '

He looked to me for support. I said, 'Right,' in a neutral voice, trying to convey that I understood without necessarily agreeing.

Nathan finished his bottle and held it above his head. 'Same again, hon,' he told the waitress. I hoped it wasn't going to end up on our bill. 'The thing about women,' he said, using his finger to emphasize his words, 'is they put men in boxes. And, for Louise, I was always the good-looking guy she could show off at parties and say, "See what I've got." '

I wasn't sure about this. When Nathan's hair had started receding years ago, he'd responded by shaving it all off. His crown was now covered with a dark fuzz. I'm sure he thought this made him look like a tough guy, but his pale blue eyes were a little too sensitive for that. The stubble around his jaw was paler with some white at the chin. He was in better shape than when I'd last seen him. It seemed that splitting from Louise had been his cue to go back to the gym. His arms and chest looked well-toned while his belly had flattened out. He looked good for a man in his early forties, but it wasn't like every woman in the place was gazing at him in awe.

I thought back to all the times we'd had with Nathan and Louise. They laughed and joked together one time we spent a few days at the beach. I would have said they looked like two people in love who were also good friends. But, I reflected, I was the last person who should have been surprised by the differences between a couple's public and private life. People who saw Tina and me together would have thought we were a normal husband and wife. They wouldn't believe I'd often licked another man's cum off her chest and once oiled up her asshole to prepare it for her lover's cock.

'It would never occur to a woman that someone who looks like me might have other qualities, as well,' said Nathan. 'Might be dynamic enough to pick her up in the car, for instance. Might know how to get a key out of a lock. Might—would you believe?—have a brain. But, no, she has her family to help her, her friends to talk to, and me to hang on her arm, looking pretty.'

'I don't think all women are like that,' I said, gently.

He turned on me with a sardonic look. 'So you satisfy all Tina's needs? She doesn't need anyone else?'

This clearly wasn't the case and I wished I'd kept quiet.

'Two can play that game,' said Nathan. 'In future, if I need any help or if I want to talk to someone, I'll go to the guys.' I looked over at the table where Nathan had been sitting. One of the men was trying to drink two bottles of beer at the same time while his friends hammered the table to urge him on. I couldn't imagine discussing my feelings and problems with them, but maybe they had their more sensitive moments.

'What about … Caitlin?' asked Tina. 'Does *she* need you?'

Nathan shook his head. 'I had to dump her. She started saying she'd leave her husband to be with me. That's not what it was about.' He took a long pull on his bottle and said sadly, 'I'm still in love with Louise. That's not going to change.' The cynical look came back into his eyes. 'That's the other problem with women: they don't understand that some relationships are purely physical. There are times when I'm not looking for a partner. I'm just looking for a fuck.' He eyed Charlotte again. 'And on that subject, are you free tomorrow night?'

Charlotte shook her head. 'Appointment at the STD clinic.'

I don't think he heard her, because he promised, 'I'll call you some time.' Standing up, he said, 'I'd better go back to the guys. Think about what I've said.' He hadn't said anything deserving thought, but I nodded vaguely as he walked away.

'I don't think I like your friend,' said Charlotte, with a scowl.

'I don't think we like him at the moment,' I said, looking to Tina for confirmation, but she was staring at the table and chewing her lower lip.

Charlotte shook her head like she was trying to dismiss Nathan from her mind. She took out her phone and tapped the screen several times. 'What are you guys doing tomorrow?' she asked.

Tina raised her head. 'We aren't doing anything, are we, babe?'

'I don't think so.'

'There's a club night at Pandora's Box. If you want to see what it's like, I'll take you along.'

Chapter Five

~

Partially hidden between a convenience store and an office building was a short tunnel leading to a small, walled courtyard. In one of the walls was a heavy, black door. Leading the way confidently, Charlotte banged on the door with the side of her fist. I half-expected a hatch to open and a face to appear, demanding the password. But a large man with a black goatee emerged through the door. His forbidding face split into a grin when he saw who was outside. 'Charlotte!' he said, bending forward to give her a peck on the cheek. 'You've been gone too long, my angel!'

'I've been busy,' said Charlotte. Since I'd known her, she'd spent most evenings chatting, reading, or watching DVDs, so I suspected this wasn't the real reason she'd stayed away.

'A few familiar faces in there, I'm sure,' said the man, giving her a pointed look which made me uneasy.

Charlotte grunted noncommittally before turning to us. 'This is Rob and Tina. They're two of my favorite people on earth. Let's look after them, okay?'

'My name's Derek,' he told us. 'If anyone gives you any shit, you shout for me and I'll unleash hell. Got that?'

We smiled gratefully and he ushered us in. Each of us

had a bag containing our costume for the evening. He shone his torch into them and looked satisfied we weren't carrying anything illegal. Charlotte went to the desk inside to pay and sign the register. I wondered if this was the sort of place where people signed in as Dark Mistress or Tina's Cuckold, but Charlotte used her real name, so we did too. I handed over a large amount of money to the woman behind the desk, and we followed Charlotte down a flight of stairs.

As we descended, I could smell damp. That, added to a growing claustrophobia and uncomfortable heat, made me think this was the least erotic place on earth. But Charlotte and Tina were taking the steps quickly. They weren't thinking of turning back. At the bottom of the stairs, Charlotte stopped and waited for me to catch them up. 'I've had a thought,' she said. 'What are we trying to do tonight?'

'What do you mean?' I asked.

But Tina understood what Charlotte was asking. 'It's mainly a fact find. But if anything looks interesting, I could be tempted to join in.'

Nodding, Charlotte pushed open a set of double doors and we went in. The damp was masked by strong perfumes and colognes. But there was also a hint of sweat in the air. As we stepped in, I felt even more claustrophobic. Many people in the room were wearing only the skimpiest clothes, so I shouldn't have been surprised the heat was turned up so high.

Charlotte and Tina went to the ladies' room to change. Going in to the men's room, I was confronted by a guy changing out of a sober gray suit into a powder blue mini dress with stockings and suspenders. Another had taken off jeans and a t-shirt and was putting on black leather trousers. He had nothing on his upper body except a bow tie and top hat. I found an empty square yard of floor where I could change. I've never felt less self-conscious taking off my clothes in front of other men. In a room full of guys dressed as extras from *The Rocky Horror Show*, who was going to notice me in my shorts? I put my jeans and sweater in my bag and changed into the tuxedo. It wasn't easy to get near the mirror but, when I did see myself, I thought I looked pretty cool. A man in a red rubber t-shirt looked at me and said, 'Shaken not shtirred,' in his best Sean Connery voice.

I waited for Tina and Charlotte outside the bathrooms. I felt more comfortable now I was in a light jacket. I was sorry for the people encased in rubber or leather. Maybe they explained the tang of sweat in the air. I overheard two people talking. A guy in a leather waistcoat was telling a woman—I *think* it was a woman—in a pink babydoll, 'You know, if you're looking to change your mortgage provider, I should be able to help.' I found this strangely comforting. Under the costumes, these were people with normal lives and the same boring concerns I had.

I looked around. I didn't know what the building upstairs had been originally, but the club had the look of a converted storage area. The ceilings were low with arched entrances leading to other rooms. I'd expected a BDSM club to be dark and shadowy. But the walls were red brick. This, combined with a red filter on some of the lights, gave the room a rosy glow and I could see everything clearly. I recognized The Cure and Depeche Mode playing in the background, but it was quiet enough for people to talk easily.

A woman led a fat man with white hair through the club by a length of rope tied loosely round his neck. He was wearing nothing except normal-looking brown trousers. The top half of his face was covered by a plastic pig mask. As if this weren't clear enough, he had the word "PIG" written across his substantial belly in red lipstick. But the visible part of his face showed a broad grin. When he had his back to me, I noticed his trousers had been modified, with a section cut out of the back to expose his butt. A curly pink tail was wedged between his cheeks. I imagined the punishment would be severe if he relaxed and let it fall out.

Charlotte and Tina came out of the ladies'. I looked at them for a moment with my mouth open. Charlotte was stunning in a red leather basque, tight black hot pants, fishnet stockings and high-heeled patent leather shoes. Tina also looked good in a short black dress. Around her neck was a collar, which I recognized. When I'd bought it, I'd assumed Boris would wear it, but it suited Tina surprisingly well. It was attached to Boris's spare leash. Charlotte held the handle. 'Let me show you around,' she said. 'It doesn't look like the place has changed much since I was here last.'

I followed as she led Tina under one of the arches and into a large circular room. At one side was a curved bar, with tables in front of it. The rest of the room was empty floor, painted black with colored lights flashing above it. It had the forlorn look that empty dance floors always have. Against the back wall was a long wooden bench with ominous-looking leather straps dangling at its sides. 'This is a good place to start,' said Charlotte. 'You can have a drink and watch what's going on. It should liven up soon. People often come here when they arrive, to show off the outfit they've been working on all week. And they have demonstrations here most nights.'

'Fifty ways to punish your lover?' I suggested, only half-joking.

'That sort of thing,' Charlotte replied, seriously. 'You'll also see some spanking and caning. If subs have spoken to their doms disrespectfully or haven't been dancing well enough or some other trumped-up charge, they find themselves in trouble. They're put against a wall and punished. But nothing too extreme goes on here.' She took us to another black door. 'The harder stuff is in the dungeon, on the next level down.' She stopped and looked at us. 'Maybe you don't want to see this, your first time.'

I thought she might have a point, but Tina said, 'I'm not here to dip my toes. Let's dive in.'

We went down another flight of stairs. After we reached the bottom, we found ourselves in another room. It was like everything had been turned up a notch. Here, the walls and ceiling *were* black. A more pungent smell of sweat mingled with stronger perfumes and colognes. And everyone had a more determined look. These people weren't here to discuss mortgages: they meant business. I also noticed the smell of cigarette smoke. There were no-smoking signs upstairs but here, it seemed, people made their own rules. A woman with dark curly hair spilling out from her Catwoman hood lounged in a leather armchair. A fully-clothed man knelt at her feet. She drew luxuriously on a long cigarette and flicked it into the man's mouth. He showed her the ash on his tongue, closed his mouth, and swallowed. 'Thank you for allowing me to serve you, mistress,' he said. She drew on the cigarette again and flicked it at his crotch. The ash wasn't still burning so couldn't do any damage, but he seemed to enjoy the symbolism of it. There was an impressive bulge in his trousers for her to aim at.

Bolted to the back wall was a large wooden X, with a naked woman tied to it. A man with a black beard whipped her back and ass. 'Please, no more,' she said. 'I promise I'll be good.' The man took no notice and kept on plying his whip. Red welts were standing out on her pale skin. A group of people stood around, watching. It should have been a disturbing scene, but wasn't. She was laughing as she begged him to stop. Finally, she said, 'Green eggs and ham.'

The man lowered his whip immediately. Taking a small bottle out of his pocket, he tenderly rubbed lotion into the marks on her skin. 'You did well,' he told her.

'So did you,' she replied. 'That was the best you've ever been.' It was like two musicians congratulating each other on a successful concert.

At the end of the room farthest from the door, a man was standing calmly with his legs apart. He was wearing nothing but a black shirt, which he held above his waist, away from his cock and balls. Five women were lined up, facing him. They took it in turns to run forward and kick him in the groin. They talked about who was winning. I wondered if they were scoring each other on their technique. After a minute, I worked out how the game was played. A woman scored a point if the man fell to the floor or dropped to his knees after her kick. If he stayed on his feet, she got nothing.

The punishments *were* more extreme here, but I didn't get the impression people were doing anything they didn't want to do. The feeling in the room was one of indulgence, not coercion. But I couldn't imagine myself taking part in any of these activities. I thought I was better suited to the room upstairs and was pleased when Charlotte said, 'Have you seen enough?'

As we turned to go back, I noticed another door with a fire extinguisher beside it and a green Fire Exit sign above it. I liked the idea that health and safety were important, even in a torture chamber.

We found a free table by the bar in the circular room upstairs. The wooden bench had been moved to the middle of the floor. 'There's going to be a show,' said Charlotte.

'Why don't you get us a drink, babe?' said Tina.

'What does one have in a place like this?' I wondered. 'I feel I should be drinking absinthe.'

'You have that if you want, sweetie,' said Charlotte. 'I'll have a beer.'

'Usual for me,' said Tina.

I came back from the bar with two beers and a glass of white wine.

The lights dimmed over the tables and a spotlight shone on the wooden bench. A man was brought on. The only thing he wore was a black leather hood. I couldn't feel too sorry for him. As he walked, his cock was bobbing in front of him, hard and straight. The woman with him wasn't dressed like a traditional dominatrix. She was wearing a turquoise dress with short sleeves. A diamond-shaped panel was cut out of the front to reveal her cleavage. A militaristic cap in the same color marked her out as dominant. She had broad shoulders and muscles that made her look strong but not butch. Her blonde hair was tied up in an austere bun. She had a long, straight nose and piercing azure eyes. Her thin-lipped mouth was partially covered by a hands-free microphone. 'Good evening!' she shouted, extra loudly to attract attention. Her voice was deep enough to be a man's but had a feminine breathiness. The people at the tables stopped talking and turned to look at her.

In the chair beside me, Charlotte went rigid. I put my hand on her arm and whispered, 'Are you okay?' but I don't know if she heard me.

'Welcome to Pandora's Box,' said the woman. 'My name is Madame Toxic. This is my slave. It doesn't have a name. Tonight, I will be showing you how to punish a man. I use the term loosely, of course.' She turned her slave around so his back was to the audience. 'Now, men are designed to be easily punished. God has given them a butt which sticks out for caning and a broad back for whipping.' This was unorthodox theology, but I didn't think it wise to argue with her. She turned him back. 'But we're not focusing on that today. Slaves are generally useless, but you can get some entertainment from the ridiculous collection of bits they keep between their legs. The balls, in particular, are very sensitive, making them perfect for punishment. Even a gentle squeeze will produce a satisfying wince.' The women in the audience sat up, interested, while the men—even those who were obviously submissive—crossed their legs anxiously.

She patted the bench with her right hand and said, 'On.' He climbed onto the bench and lay on his back. She turned to the audience again and pointed at the leather straps. 'Some people like to tie the slave to the bench. But I never do. I believe the force of my personality is enough to keep my slave exactly where I want it.' She spoke directly into the man's face. 'You wouldn't dream of moving without permission, would you?'

'Never, mistress,' he said, emphatically.

'Now, I prefer to start slow,' she said. Her slave's erect cock was an uncut seven inches, giving the lie to a common myth about all submissive men. She pulled down his foreskin to expose the plum-colored head. 'As I'm warming up, I like to flick the head. Many slaves have told me this doesn't hurt as such, but it's an unpleasant sensation. The important thing is there's no pleasure in it for the slave. Now, moving back to the balls, you may be familiar with the song, "Twist and Shout." But possibly you don't know its true meaning, which is: take a slave's balls and twist them until it shouts.'

She grabbed his scrotum in her right hand and twisted it sharply. She wasn't surprised when he didn't make a sound. 'You see, no reaction. This is a common problem. If you've been punishing a slave for a long time, its balls get as hard as lumps of coal and more difficult to hurt. When this happens, you have two choices. You can throw your slave out like the piece of trash it is or you can move on to something more advanced. I may well be discarding this slave soon, but, for now, I will show you other things you can do.' She put the fingers and thumb of her left hand around the point where his scrotum joined to his body. Squeezing hard, she said, 'Note the way this smooths out all the wrinkles in the sack and makes the balls themselves stand out all pink and shiny. There's no doubt what the target is here. There are three things you can do. You can slap the balls with the flat of your hand.' She illustrated this. A smacking sound rang out round the room but still there was no reaction in the slave's face. 'You can use the back of your hand for a nice percussive crack of the nails on the sensitive little globes. Or you can decide the fun and games are over and it's time for some *serious pain*.' She balled her fist and held it up to show the audience. Holding the slave's balls tight and defenseless in her left hand, she punched them hard with her right. This time, there wasn't a smacking sound. It was the sickening thud of a hard object hitting a soft one. The men groaned in sympathy. We could imagine how the slave felt. But all he did was let out a little cry of anguish. He didn't move or flinch in any way. She looked at his face—maybe to check he was all right, maybe to enjoy his torment. She punched his balls again. A little more softly this time. But there was still that dull thud. He cried out more loudly, but still stayed exactly where his mistress wanted him. 'All slaves know that orgasms are a privilege. You are well within your rights to keep your slave restrained in such a way that it never cums. But, if you do graciously decide to grant your slave an orgasm, you must make sure the experience is painful rather than pleasurable.' She reached into the pocket of her dress and pulled out two lengths of string, which she held up to the audience. 'Ordinary string. Any kind will do. A thin rope works as well.'

She tied one length of string around the base of his ball sack, the other around the base of his cock. She pulled both strings so tight that the man grimaced. Taking his cock in her hand, she jerked it hard. 'Sometimes, the slave won't be able to cum at all and this will cause a painful obstruction in its body.' This sounded like another version of the blocked orgasm Tina had given me. 'Other times, it will be able to ejaculate, but the strain of pushing the cum through the bonds will maximize the pain while reducing pleasure to zero.'

His face contorted as she yanked his cock. Nothing happened for three or four seconds, then a splash of cum was forced out of him under such pressure that it shot six feet in the air. 'Now,' she said, 'this is the most important thing.' She pumped his cock even more forcibly. 'After it's cum, you must continue to pull its cock as hard as possible. There won't be any trace of pleasure left. It'll be pure pain, pure punishment.'

This was the moment when I really felt for the guy. I knew something as gentle as having my cock sucked was uncomfortable when I'd just cum. I couldn't imagine what he was going through.

After a minute of this, the show ended. The man got off the bench and bowed to the audience. He walked off with his cock and balls still tied up. The mistress was not the type to bow to anyone. She told the audience, 'Remember what I've taught you,' and followed her slave.

The lights came back up over the seating area. 'What did you think?' I asked Tina.

'Do we have any string at home?' she replied.

I turned to Charlotte. 'Did you learn anything new or was

it all old stuff for you?'

Gazing fixedly at the empty stage, she didn't answer. I thought maybe she was reminded of something bad that had happened to her. I put a supportive arm around her waist and felt her body stiffen again as Madame Toxic walked across the floor. I hadn't expected her to do a meet and greet with the audience. She headed straight for our table with her eyes locked on Charlotte. I should have realized who she was a lot earlier. 'Let's get out of here!' I hissed, trying to lift Charlotte out of her seat. But, small as she was, I couldn't move her.

'Hello, Charlotte.' Even without the microphone, her voice was deep and authoritative.

'Natalie,' responded Charlotte, tonelessly.

'Did you enjoy the demonstration?'

'Very educational,' said Charlotte, drily.

'I'm not sure it was my best work. I'm still getting to grips with how to treat a male slave. I'd prefer to show the good mistresses and masters what I do with a little slut like you. Why don't you come and work for me?'

'I'm not looking for a new job at the moment.'

'You still handing out keys at the hotel? A job that could be done by a vending machine?'

'It's fine,' said Charlotte.

'Fine?' echoed Natalie, contemptuously. 'We know what that means. "You look fine" is another way of saying, "You look like shit but I don't have the guts to say it." When was the last time you were so turned on your heart was hammering and you couldn't catch your breath?' Charlotte didn't answer. Natalie gestured in our direction. 'Do you think someone like you could ever be happy with the dinner party crowd?'

She obviously didn't know what went on at *our* dinner parties.

'These are my friends,' said Charlotte.

'Friends?' Natalie laughed—a horrible, hacking laugh. 'As if people like us need friends.'

'Maybe it's what I need right now.'

'*I'm* the one you need,' said Natalie, pointing to her own chest. 'Come with me. We have things to talk about.'

'We were just leaving,' I said.

But Charlotte stood up. 'I'll just have a quick word with Natalie,' she said. 'You guys stay here. I won't be long.' Natalie didn't try to suppress her look of triumph as she strode away across the floor. Charlotte looked at us for a second, then gave the handle of the leash to me. 'You're Rob's slave now,' she told Tina.

'In his dreams,' said Tina, giving me a sideways look.

I put my hand on Charlotte's wrist. 'Talking *about* Natalie makes you cry. Why on earth would you want to talk *to* her?'

She gently pushed my hand away. 'I'll be fine, sweetie, don't worry.' She ran after Natalie like an obedient puppy.

Not knowing what else to do, we sat and waited. I felt like we'd been abandoned in a foreign country by the only person who could speak the language. There were plenty of eye-catching people in the room, but I didn't want to look up in case they tried to engage with me and I wouldn't know what to do. Tina sat beside me looking like a slave who was increasingly annoyed with her life of servitude. Neither of us had thought to bring a watch to a BDSM club, so we didn't know how long we waited there.

Standing up, I said, 'I'll see if I can find her.'

'You can't leave me here alone,' said Tina.

'Come on, then, we'll go together.'

I thought leading my wife around on a chain would make me feel powerful. But being with Tina in a place like this made me nervous, because I knew I'd have to protect her if anything went wrong. Not that there was any sign of things going wrong. People were being punished while others watched, but I didn't feel anyone was being hassled. I noticed a woman with her panties round her knees. Another woman was wearing a pair of gardening gloves. She carefully plucked stinging nettles from their stalk and laid them in the gusset of the other woman's panties. I had a good idea what was going to happen next and, in other circumstances, would have stayed to watch, but we had to move on.

We searched everywhere. A couple of times, I saw someone I thought was Charlotte, but the gothic look was popular among the women, with black a favorite color for hair and makeup. We ventured back to the dungeon, where a naked man was sitting on a hard chair. There was a contraption fastened to his balls which reminded me of an old-fashioned tennis racket press. Two parallel wooden slats were separated by a bolt at either end. As the woman with him turned the screws, the slats squeezed his balls more tightly. He grunted with pain, but far from telling the woman to stop, he kept saying, 'More, more.' The woman's eyes were wide with delight, but she also bit her lip nervously. It looked like she enjoyed punishing him, but was worried about going too far.

There was still no sign of Charlotte, so we went up both flights of stairs until we reached the main entrance. Derek recognized us and asked, 'Having a good time?'

I shook my head. 'We've lost Charlotte.'

He didn't look surprised. 'Natalie?' he asked. I nodded. 'I'll see if I can find them.' He went off, leaving us standing awkwardly inside the front door. He came back a few minutes later, shaking his head. 'Someone said they left half an hour ago.'

IN THE TAXI ON the way home, I texted Charlotte, *Are you OK?*

She still hadn't replied by the time we arrived. It was only ten o'clock, but Tina and I were both tired. I let Boris out the back door and made a cup of tea for us to take to bed. I was checking my phone for the twentieth time when I heard a tut behind me. 'She went of her own accord,' said Tina.

'I know,' I said. 'But Natalie's not good for her.'

Tina put her hands on my shoulders. 'Sweetie,' she said, deliberately using Charlotte's favorite word, 'you're not her dad.'

Chapter Six

~

WHEN I WOKE UP on Saturday morning, the first thing I did was check my phone again. All I wanted was a single line from Charlotte saying, *Don't worry, I'm all right.* There was nothing.

At half past nine, Boris barked once before wagging his tail, telling us the mail had arrived. I went out to get it. In amongst the bills and advertisements was a handwritten envelope addressed to Tina. It was stiffer than a letter so I guessed it was a card, but it was still six weeks until Christmas. I went back inside and handed it to her. She raised her eyebrows. 'Maybe it's from Aunt Emily. She likes to send her cards early.' Looking more closely at the envelope, she said, 'It's not her writing, though. I wonder who it's from.'

'If only there were some way of finding out,' I said.

'Fuck off, Rob,' she said, with a smile. She opened the envelope and read the card. Giggling, she passed it to me.

"Dear Tina (and Rob)," it began. It always made me feel so good when I was put in parentheses, like I was a bit player in the Tina show. "Sorry for being such an industrial strength asshole on Thursday. You no doubt realized I was slightly drunk. Seeing you guys reminded me of the good times the four of us used to have back in the day. I was angry and sad. But that's no excuse for the things I said. Please could you say sorry to your friend? She seems nice and didn't deserve some drunk guy harassing her. I hope I can make it up to you and we can still be friends. Apologies again, Nathan."

'Nice of him to write that,' I said. 'We probably would have given him a second chance, anyway.'

Tina wasn't listening. She had her phone out and was busy texting. After she'd sent it, she showed me the screen. *Come round at 8 tonight with a nice bottle of Pinot and all will be forgiven.* I handed the phone back to her and said, 'Is that a good idea? How's Louise going to feel if she hears we're hanging out with Nathan—fraternizing with the enemy?'

'We'll have to make sure she doesn't find out.' She paused and gave me the wicked look I knew so well. 'Because she won't be happy if she finds out what I'm planning for Nathan.'

'What do you …?' My stomach dropped. 'Oh no, Tina, you're not thinking—'

'I sure am,' she said. 'I want to ask him over and sound him out. What's the worst that could happen?'

Never ask an over-thinker that question. I immediately thought of twenty scenarios that would land us all in hospital or prison. The determination in Tina's eyes told me there wasn't much point in arguing. Nevertheless, I tried. 'We don't want to lose our dogsitter.'

'Is that the best you've got?' asked Tina, with a pitying smile.

'Okay … you remember what we said after things went wrong with Steve? You'd never start anything with a colleague again.'

'I don't work with Nathan,' said Tina.

I clicked my tongue impatiently. 'But a friend is even worse. I've always thought cuckold relationships were complicated enough without throwing friendship into the mix.'

'I think it's a good idea. Someone we know. Someone we trust. And I've always had a bit of a thing for him.'

'Have you?' I'd never noticed any spark between them.

'Oh yes. He's a good-looking guy. I was always jealous of Louise.'

'Yes. Remember her? Your friend, Louise? Sisters before misters.' I wasn't sure if that was a saying, but it sounded like it could be.

'It's not like they're still together.'

'But he's still in love with her. He said so.'

'Good. He won't fall in love with me, then. We can just have some fun.'

'And it's pretty obvious she's still in love with him.'

'So we make sure she doesn't find out.'

We were going round in circles. So I tried a new approach. 'Thursday was like being trapped in a room with a drunk frat boy who's just been dumped. *That's* the kind of guy you want in your life?'

'That's not the way I saw it. To me, he was a man with a lot of anger inside him.'

'The *last* sort of person you want to get involved with.'

She smiled knowingly. 'You mean the *first*.'

'Charlotte said BDSM has nothing to do with anger.'

'All I know is you gave me the best spanking of my life when you were angry.' I regretted admitting that to her. It's possible to be *too* open with someone. 'I want to do this, babe,' she said. 'It feels right.' I didn't say anything and looked away. But I could feel her eyes on me as she said, 'You do trust me, don't you, Rob?'

'Of course I do,' I replied, automatically. But, as I said it, I was hit with the sad truth that, after everything that had happened, I didn't trust her anymore. I could no longer be sure she had the best interests of Rob and Tina at heart.

THAT EVENING, TINA DRESSED in a pair of tight jeans and a black blouse with a neckline which showed off an inch of cleavage. I was fairly sure she wasn't wearing anything under it. Sexy, but not trying too hard.

At eight o'clock exactly, the doorbell rang. Tina opened the door to find Nathan standing outside with a bottle of wine in one hand and a bunch of flowers in the other. I'd never seen anyone who looked less like a stern master. Even as he came in, he was apologizing. 'Guys, I am so sorry. I don't know what was wrong with me. These words were pouring out of my mouth. Part of my brain was screaming, "Shut up, Nathan! Stop talking!" But the rest of my brain was too drunk to listen. Thank you so much for inviting me round and giving me the chance to—'

Tina kissed him on the lips. She didn't normally do this. He looked surprised, but probably thought she was kissing him to shut him up. He came up to me. We shook hands and he asked, 'Can you forgive me, Rob?'

'Of course,' I said, but I wasn't sure I'd forgive him if he did the things my wife wanted him to do.

Tina and Nathan sat on the couch in the den. I went into the kitchen and sighed as I took three wine glasses out of the cupboard. How many times had I done this before? Going back to the den, I poured the wine. 'To reconciliation?' Nathan suggested as a toast.

'To new beginnings,' said Tina. We all clinked glasses together. 'Where are you living at the moment?' she asked him.

'I was lucky there,' he replied. 'I split from Louise just as a guy in my team moved to the Beijing office. He had to rent out his apartment in a hurry, so I got a good deal. A two bedroom place on the top floor with a great view of the city. It's only twenty minutes from here. You guys should come round some time.'

'That would be nice,' said Tina. 'How's … your work going?' I could tell she didn't care about his apartment or his work and was filling in time while she thought of the right things to say. Tina had always found this part of the cuckolding life difficult. It's never easy to tell a man you want him to fuck you while your husband watches. It's even harder to say you want to use him to act out your BDSM fantasies. When he'd finished talking about work, Tina folded her hands and began, 'Nathan, when we talked in the pub … you sounded mad at Louise.'

He held up his hands. 'It was the beer talking.'

'I heard some genuine anger there.'

He leaned forward, looking grave. 'Tina, if you think I'm going to hurt your friend in some way, you have nothing to worry about.'

'That's good to know,' she said, with a little smile. 'But you clearly have this rage somewhere inside you. We were … wondering if you'd like … an outlet of some sort.'

'I don't follow,' he said, shaking his head.

Tina backed up a little. 'Rob and I have a slightly unusual relationship.'

'What's a *usual* relationship?' he asked, wryly.

'Good point, but … do you know what a cuckold is?'

'Sure. It's when a man's wife is unfaithful to him.'

'And he's happy about it,' she added. 'That's important. A cuckold and a hot wife agree that she can have sex with other men because it turns them both on. And, well … that's me and Rob. He's only happy when I'm having sex with another man.'

'Really?' he asked me, looking surprised.

I nodded. 'It's our thing.'

'It's *one* of our things,' said Tina. 'Recently, we've been thinking of getting into something else.' She looked at the ceiling and I could see her mind working. 'Last night, Charlotte—the girl you met on Thursday—took us to one of those bondage and discipline clubs.'

At the mention of Charlotte, I instinctively looked at my phone. There was still no word from her. Meanwhile, Nathan looked puzzled, as if he wasn't sure where this was leading.

'It was interesting,' continued Tina, 'but no one there was my type. They were all treating it as a game.' This wasn't true. Some of the people I'd seen were laughing, but because they were enjoying themselves, not because they weren't taking it seriously. Most had looked committed to what they were doing. 'If I allowed someone to … do anything like that to me,' she said, 'there would have to be emotional content. He wants to give me pleasure, but, underneath that, there has to be something more—a desire to hurt. And someone with real anger inside them might just be the right person.'

'So, you want me to …?' he began, uncertainly.

Tina took a deep breath. 'We were hoping you'd like to … explore certain aspects of … punishment and domination.' She looked away and added quietly, 'With me.'

Nathan looked too stunned to say anything. He finally managed an, 'I see.'

'You don't have to give us an answer immediately,' she said. 'And if you're not interested, that's fine. No hard feelings. But please don't say anything to Louise.'

'I *am* interested,' he said, quickly. 'And if you were some stranger who'd told me that in a bar, I'd have you over my knee right now, but ….'

She guessed what was worrying him. 'But we're friends.'

'Exactly,' he said.

'And we'll still be friends, whether we do this or not.'

'Will we?' he asked. 'Can we chat over dinner after doing … something like this?'

'Have you never stayed friends with an ex?' she asked.

'I've tried, but it's never lasted. You only realize how much of the conversation was, "I love you," and "I can't believe I'm with someone so great," when you can't say things like that anymore.'

'That won't be a problem for us. We've always had plenty to say to each other.'

'But if it turns out to be a disaster, can we agree we won't mention it again and go back to how things were?' Tina gave an almost imperceptible wiggle. I was sure he didn't notice it, but I recognized it as triumphant. She'd interpreted his words as acquiescence. 'I've always been fascinated by this sort of thing,' he added. 'I've some experience, but not much.'

'My last lover introduced me to certain parts of it, but I'm not exactly an expert myself. We can learn together. Just because you're the dominant or the top or whatever you want to call yourself, don't think it's all on your shoulders. You don't have to come up with all the ideas and stage manage everything yourself. We can discuss what we're going to do. Besides, I think it's kinky if I tell you how I want you to hurt and humiliate me. I like the idea of plotting my own downfall. And one important thing: I don't just want you to hurt my body; I want it to be a mindfuck, as well.'

'How do you mean?'

'Well, one minute act like I'm the sexiest goddess who's ever lived, the next make me believe I'm an ugly skank no one would ever want. Note I said "make me believe," not just "tell me." '

'That shouldn't be … too hard,' he began, tentatively. 'I've … always thought you were good enough to fuck, but not to date.'

I could see a flash of the boorish sexism he'd shown in the bar. But then he looked at her, as if he wasn't sure whether she'd kiss him or slap his face. What she did was smile encouragingly and say, 'Yes, that's good. You've got the right idea. Now, how do I compare with Louise?'

I thought he might be uncomfortable, talking about his wife in this context, but, instead, he was getting into his stride. He said, 'You're better-looking than her, but she is so much sexier.'

Tina purred with pleasure. 'Excellent. Keeping it real. Exactly what we want.' She looked serious again and said, 'Now, this is important. I want you to remember the word, *Marquis*. This is our safe word. It stops everything immediately. If I say, "You're hurting me," or, "Don't do that," or, "Please, no more," you keep going. Better still, laugh and call me names. But if you hear *Marquis*, we stop and talk about what's gone wrong.'

He frowned. 'Why *Marquis*?'

'I've been reading up on this topic, looking at a lot of websites. Although I'm interested in sadism, I think the dear old Marquis de Sade himself went *too far*. I don't want you dropping me into a vat of boiling oil.'

'I'll make a note of that,' he said.

'So if I say the word, *Marquis*, it means, *Too far*.'

'Got it,' he said.

'And one more thing,' said Tina. 'I don't mind hearing "dirty whore" or "cheap slut" at the height of passion, but otherwise call me Tina, not slave. And I'll call you Nathan. I haven't used the word "sir" since I was at school and "master" always reminds me of *I Dream of Jeannie* reruns.'

'Fine.'

'What do you say we try something now?'

'Right now? Er … like what?'

'Would you like to see my tits?'

He seemed excited by this idea, but then remembered the role he was playing and tried to look indifferent. 'I saw most of them when we went to the beach and you wore the yellow bikini. Your tits didn't look like anything special.'

Tina gave a little moan. 'But wouldn't you like me to show them to you in front of my husband?' She looked up at me. 'What do you think of my breasts, Rob?'

'Best I've ever seen,' I replied.

'You need to get out more,' said Nathan. He turned back to Tina. 'Unbutton your blouse and tell me why you're doing it.'

She undid her top two buttons. 'I'm doing it to excite you. I want you to be sexually attracted to me.'

'But you're Rob's wife. You should only want to excite him.'

'I'm not just a wife. I'm a *hot* wife. Rob belongs to me. I belong to men … and maybe women, as well, but that's another story. Let me tell you something. The night Louise went out and ended up in bed with that young guy—did you know I was with her?'

A cloud passed over Nathan's face. 'No, I didn't know that.'

'She was mad at you for cheating, and wanted revenge.' She paused and looked at him steadily. 'I was with her, encouraging her to cheat on you. I spotted the guy and introduced them to each other. It's my fault your wife cheated on you.'

I'd never seen anyone turn so angry that quickly. I could

tell Tina was a little frightened by what she'd unleashed, but also turned on. 'You fucking bitch,' said Nathan, in a low, threatening voice.

She taunted him, 'Yes, I'm a fucking bitch. Another man got to see Louise's body.' Her lip curled as she added, 'The body you find so much sexier than mine. He put his stupid face between her tits. She opened up her pussy, and showed what was waiting for him. She's your wife. Her pussy's supposed to be just for you. But it was his that night. And you know what he said about her? That she was good enough to fuck, but not to date.'

I didn't see how he could be any angrier, and I thought she was playing a dangerous game by continuing to goad him. 'Get your tits out,' he said through clenched teeth. She undid the remaining buttons and took the blouse off. She sat there, topless. He gave her tits an appraising look. 'They're not as good as Louise's,' he said.

'They're bigger,' she retorted.

'But hers are the perfect shape and size. And she has gorgeous nipples. Not like yours.'

'That's good,' she said, with a smile. 'Now, put your finger and thumb around my left nipple and twist it until I say stop.' When he'd turned her nipple thirty degrees clockwise, she said 'Hold it there. Now, that's as far as you can go without hurting me. If you don't want to hurt me, let go. If you want to hear me cry with pain and know you caused it, twist some more. It's your choice.'

There wasn't any doubt which choice he'd make. He twisted her nipple hard. She gasped at the sudden pain. Their eyes met and I saw a connection between them I hadn't seen with any of her other lovers. Steve had aroused her physically. Adam had used his mentalist tricks to get inside her head. This was something else. The look said, *We understand each other.*

They held this gaze for over a minute. All the time, he maintained the painful pressure on her nipple. Then she brushed his hand away and said, 'That's enough for tonight.'

His face fell as she stood up and put her blouse back on. For someone who was supposed to be the submissive in this relationship, she was asserting a lot of control. He stood up unsteadily, unable to hide the large bulge in his trousers. She put her hand on it and said, 'Take your hard-on back to your apartment, and think about everything we've discussed tonight. Then give me a ring tomorrow and we'll talk over some ideas.'

She walked him to the door. 'I think we're going to have fun together,' she said. She put her arms around his neck and kissed him on the lips.

'Okay, speak to you tomorrow,' he mumbled, and went out.

Closing the door behind him, Tina said, 'I have a good feeling about this.'

I sat on the couch where Nathan had been. 'But Charlotte said—'

Tina held up her hand. 'I'm not Charlotte. And I don't like being compared to someone else.' She realized immediately she couldn't back this up and added, 'Not in this way.'

I slumped in my seat. I could see this playing out with depressing familiarity. 'So here we go again,' I said. 'Nathan's going to come round on a Friday night and fuck you. Maybe he'll spank you, call you a whore, and say your tits aren't as good as Louise's. But essentially, he'll be here to fuck you. And everything will be fine for a while. But then something will happen. Either you'll go off with him or it'll get too much for me and I'll have to leave.'

'You've got it all planned out, haven't you, Rob? We could try learning from the past and not repeating the same mistakes.'

'How?'

She thought for a while. 'I'm not sure I want this to be a regular thing. It could just be something I have to get out of my system. So how's this? The three of us have a weekend in a hotel, where there are no rules. Imagine it, Rob,' said Tina, her eyes lighting up. 'Your lovely wife giving herself totally to another man, saying, "Here's my body—do whatever you want to it. Take out all your pain and frustration on me. Think of every woman who's ever screwed you over and punish *me* for what they've done." How does that sound?'

'Risky,' I said.

'Maybe I like risk,' she responded. She put her hand on my crotch and smiled evilly as she felt my rock hard cock. 'And I'm not the only one.'

I tried to think straight. 'It's a great fantasy,' I said. 'If you want to go to bed and *talk* about it, I'm totally on board. But doing it is another matter.'

She looked at me with a stern calmness that gave me chills. 'You're not going to make me go to the dark place alone, are you, Rob? Not again?' So I was a bad husband if I *didn't* let someone hurt and humiliate my wife. 'I need you beside me. I need to know you're there, ready to protect me if things go *too far.*'

Chapter Seven

~

FOR THE NEXT TWO weeks, Nathan was working out of town, so we didn't see him. Tina acted like she was researching a doctoral thesis on BDSM. Every time I saw her, she was on her laptop, busily taking notes as she looked at websites and discussion groups. She texted Nathan several times a day, giving him the highlights of her findings. His responses were enthusiastic, but with a hint of wariness. He initially seemed reluctant for them to spend a whole weekend together. I think he was worried they'd do everything in half an hour and then pass the rest of the time in awkward silence. But he came round to the idea when he realized Tina had no shortage of things she wanted to do. He said he'd found the perfect place for us to stay.

I wasn't allowed to see everything they sent each other. Tina thought it would be more stimulating for me if I had one or two surprises.

As the time to go away approached, Tina became more and more eager. She didn't quite run downstairs to cross another day off the calendar, but on Wednesday, she looked at me excitedly and said, 'Only two days to go. Are you looking forward to it, babe?'

No was the straight answer. I felt like a middle-aged man who was prepared to forego the pleasures of getting drunk if it meant avoiding the hangover. I was still turned on by the thought of watching Tina with another man. But experience had taught me there were always consequences, which often involved me being alone. And I wasn't sure I could rely on someone like Charlotte catching me every time I fell out of my marriage. If Tina and I had agreed to give up cuckoldry, life would have been more humdrum. But, at that point, I would have taken boredom over pain.

I WAS STILL WORRIED about Charlotte. I tried phoning her so many times that I feared concern was tipping over into stalking. I went to the hotel four times. She was never at reception and the person who was always said, 'She's not working today,' and politely declined to give any more details.

I FINISHED MY LAST lesson at four o'clock on Friday. I went home and drove Boris to Louise's place. I knew we were pushing our luck outrageously. *Could you look after our dog while my wife acts out her fantasies with your husband?*

Boris seemed happy as I left. He knew Louise would look after him. I was less sanguine as I drove back to the house. I had the feeling we were getting into something dangerous. When I arrived home, I found Tina in the bedroom, packing our small suitcase. She had changed out of her work clothes and was wearing a red and white checked blouse with black jeans and black boots. She looked good—sexy, even—but it didn't look like something you'd wear for an amorous weekend away. She guessed what I was thinking and tapped the side of her head. 'When it comes to seducing a man, my mind is more effective than any little black dress.' She pulled my thoughts back to the mundane by asking, 'How many pairs of socks do you want?'

I could imagine many things going wrong this weekend, none of which involved me running out of socks. 'Two,' I said.

'Three to be safe.'

'Nathan's got the cane and the handcuffs,' she said, casually, as if telling me he was bringing something for breakfast.

'Do you have enough condoms?' I asked.

She looked up and her eyes met mine. 'No, Rob, I haven't. I'm still on the pill. Adam and I got tested a few weeks ago. We were both fine. I haven't been with anyone else since then … except Charlotte.'

'And me,' I reminded her.

'Anything you want to tell me?'

'No.'

'Well, then, there's no problem. And Nathan said he and Caitlin got tested too.'

'Do you think you can trust him?'

'I'm going to spend the weekend letting him dominate and hurt me. If I can't trust him, I'm in real trouble.'

We set off at half past five. Tina had the directions on her knee. When she wasn't telling me where to go, she chatted happily about her week at work. She might have been talking to cover her nerves, but I didn't think so. She was as relaxed and happy as someone heading off on holiday.

We drove sixty miles and then spent over an hour trying to find the place, as it was a long way from any town. Eventually, we saw a sign that read "Comfort Hotel," half-covered by a dangling branch. I turned the car off the road onto a long driveway, which finally opened up at two large, red brick buildings. I was about to park outside reception when Tina pointed to a number of small white cottages dotted across the surrounding hills. 'We're in one of those,' she said. 'Nathan wanted to find a place where no one could hear us.'

'He thinks of everything,' I said, as I steered the car onto the narrow track through the hills.

'There's his car,' she said, pointing to the farthest cottage.

In my head, I could hear a true crime show voiceover: *As the chambermaid went to the isolated cottage on Saturday morning, she couldn't have imagined the scene of horror that would greet her*. I had an urge to turn the car around, disregarding Tina's reaction as I got us out of there. I told myself not to worry. We'd known Nathan for years. He wasn't going to do anything Tina didn't want him to do.

As we parked the car, he came out to meet us. He shook hands with me, but clearly wasn't sure how to approach Tina. She rolled her eyes, stepped up to him, and kissed him on the lips. 'You don't have to be shy,' she said.

Nathan kissed her back, but looked anxious. I was used to seeing this. However much of a stud you think you are, it's always nerve-racking to be confronted by a hot wife and her cuckold husband, knowing you have to perform. 'What do you think of the place?' he asked, for want of anything better to say.

'It's lovely,' said Tina, looking out over the hills. 'Good choice.'

He took us into the kitchen and asked us to take off our shoes so we wouldn't have to clean too much before we left. We left our bags by the large wooden table and he gave us a tour, showing us the lounge, bathroom and only bedroom, which had a double bed in it.

We went back into the kitchen and had an awkward *What do we do now?* moment. Would we act like normal people and take a little walk before the evening meal or would the fucking start immediately?

Tina had learned that nudity is a good ice-breaker. Her hands went to the top button of her blouse. She paused and looked at the kitchen window. It was unlikely anyone would walk past but, even so, she said, 'Rob, could you …?' I pulled down the blind and switched on the light. She undid her buttons. Even though he'd seen her tits before, he held his breath as she took off her blouse. So did I. Despite my growing concern about the effects of the cuckold lifestyle, my heart always pounded as I watched my wife undress for another man. Tina was beautiful and sexy. She was out of my league but she'd still married me. I must have been crazy even to think of sharing her with anyone else. And yet, here she was, enjoying the open-mouthed stare of her friend as she took her clothes off. She was wearing a purple underwired bra, which pushed her breasts up and together, giving her a deep, six inch cleavage. 'What do you think?' she asked.

'They're ….' He paused and moved his gaze up to meet her eyes. 'Do you want me to be nice or nasty about them?'

'Whatever would turn you on the most,' she said.

He looked relieved. 'They're beautiful. Can I—?'

Smiling, she held up her hand. 'Nathan, stop asking questions,' she said, gently. 'For this weekend, you can use me and my body to make all your fantasies come true. I give my consent to everything. Unless you hear the magic word, *Marquis*, do whatever you like.' Standing up, she unbuttoned her jeans and slid them down her legs, deftly removing her socks at the same time. Her panties were in the same purple material as the bra. She stood for a moment, letting him enjoy the anticipation. Then she lowered her panties slowly, revealing herself an inch at a time. Her cunt was perfectly smooth. I also noticed there wasn't even a shadow remaining of the hair she'd grown under her arms. The days of wanting her body to be attractive to me were over. I wondered if she'd asked Nathan whether he preferred smooth or hairy. My breathing quickened at the idea of my wife carefully shaving, making her body the way another man liked it.

When she was naked, she sat back on her chair, with her butt at the front of the seat. Facing Nathan, she spread her legs. 'Have a good look,' she said.

He crouched on the floor in front of her, his eyes locked on my wife's cunt. 'You shave,' he said, in a breathless whisper. 'Can I …?' he began, before stopping himself.

'She's yours, Nathan,' said Tina. 'Open her up. Put a finger inside her. I don't want you to miss anything. And part of total intimacy is knowing what I smell like and how I taste. Put your face in there. Get to know me.'

He used his thumbs to part her coral pink lips and expose the deep red of her vagina. He slid a finger inside her and moaned, 'You are so wet.'

'My turn,' she said, standing up. She put her arms around his shoulders and kissed him. This wasn't a kiss of greeting. It was exploratory. She was asking herself if she liked kissing him. It seemed she did because her lips parted. She put her hand behind his head and pulled him closer to her. He opened his mouth more and their tongues fluttered against each other. She ran her hands over his shoulders and down his arms. She'd seen him shirtless on the beach before, but this time, she was appraising him in a new way. She was her new lover rather than her friend's husband. She unbuttoned his shirt and pushed it away from his shoulders. I looked at him through Tina's eyes. He wasn't as muscular as Steve, but a little more than me. He wasn't as hairy as Mark, but he had a good patch of brown hair in the middle of his chest. Tina planted little kisses all over his chest and enjoyed burying her face in the hair. She took his right nipple into her mouth, sucked it, and closed her teeth around it. She smiled mischievously as she felt him wince. She was showing him she wasn't a pure masochist. She could inflict pain as well as take it.

The real test was still to come. Undoing his belt, she pulled down his pants and shorts. His cock was already hard. He wasn't as big as Kieran, but he was a good size—maybe seven inches and nicely thick. But it wasn't his cock that caught her attention immediately. Lifting it out of the way, she showed me his bulging sack. 'Look at Nathan's balls, Rob,' she said. 'I could go bowling with these. I couldn't even have a decent game of marbles with yours.'

Tina looked well-satisfied with what she found under Nathan's clothes. He may not have been the best in any respect, but he possibly had the best *combination* of physical qualities she looked for in a man.

'So … what first?' he asked.

Tina took a moment. I'm not sure she'd thought about this either. 'Shall we just fuck to start with? And see what happens. If anything feels natural, let's do it.'

He patted the table. 'Right now, it feels natural to bend you over this.'

Tina ran her finger along the table's square edge. 'But it would dig into me and hurt.'

'Okay,' he said. 'We can go into the bedroom.'

Tina gave him a look like he was a dim but sweet student in her class. 'But it would dig into me and hurt!' she said, more pointedly.

This time he got it. Roughly he grabbed her wrist and, turning her around, pushed her against the table. She leaned forward, supporting herself on her forearms, and parted her legs. He stood behind her and felt the entrance to her cunt with his finger. Holding his cock, he tried to place the tip in the right place. But Tina had to give him directions, 'Down a little. Slightly to the right. You're there.' He pushed his cock into her. This wasn't anything I hadn't seen before but, even so, I took a moment to appreciate Tina with another man's cock inside her. He was feeling the heat and soft moisture of my wife's vagina. He moved slowly, closing his eyes as he enjoyed the sensation. Then he seemed to remember it wasn't his job to be gentle. Grabbing hold of Tina's hips, he thrust into her hard and fast. 'That's good,' said Tina, breathing heavily. 'That's very good.'

'Yes, it is,' he agreed.

'But don't cum yet,' she said. 'I've thought of some other things I want to do.'

He pulled out of her, his cock slippery with her juices. She straightened up. The edge of the table had made a horizontal red line above her hips. They both looked at it and grinned at each other. All awkwardness had vanished and he looked at her with hungry eyes. 'What do you want?'

'Before we do anything else, I have to pee.' She moved toward the bathroom. He watched her go, but didn't move. Stopping, she looked at him over her shoulder. 'You're going to let me do it in private?'

Realizing his mistake, he started. 'No way. Privacy is a privilege which must be earned.'

He followed her into the bathroom. I was a few steps behind, wanting to see what would happen. Sitting on the toilet, she pretended to be unwilling. 'Please turn away. I can't do this with you watching.' Tina never was a great actor, and her performance was unconvincing, even when she put her hands in front of her cunt. He knelt between her legs, took hold of her wrists, and held them firmly beside her. Standing behind him, I couldn't see much, but I heard her pee hitting the bowl and splashing into the water below. He had the perfect view. It was another occasion when a man did something with my wife that I'd never done. I'd seen Tina in the bath and shower many times, but I'd always discreetly withdrawn when she wanted to use the toilet. But now Nathan was looking at my wife's cunt as urine flowed out of it. After she finished, she reached instinctively for toilet paper.

Smirking, Nathan shook his head. 'That's another privilege which must be earned.'

'But how …?' began Tina. 'Rob, I've got a job for you.' Nathan stood up and I took his place between her legs. I remembered what Charlotte had said about sex making disgusting things exciting. I was turned on by the prospect of tasting Tina's pee for the first time. I also thought this might be the only time I got near her cunt for the whole weekend, so I was going to make the most of it. I licked her from the bottom of her lips to the top. I pushed in my tongue to make sure she was clean between her lips, as well. Tina's pee reminded me of the one time I tried alcohol-free beer. There was a hint of salt and a slightly yeasty sourness. Even after I was sure I'd gotten every drop, I kept licking. I wanted at least one of her memories of this weekend to be of *me* giving her pleasure. 'Okay, that's enough,' she said, at last. Standing up, she told Nathan, 'Let's take this to the bedroom.' When we got there, she looked at the bed and said, 'There should be room for all three of us.' For his benefit, she clarified, 'When it's time to sleep, I mean. Rob might join in with some of the things we do this weekend but, for now, he's going to watch.'

I hadn't heard this, but I'd guessed as much. There was a green wicker chair in the corner of the room. I sat down, facing the bed, and waited to see what would happen. They stood by the bed and kissed again. Tina knew this simple act of affection was one of the hardest things for me to watch. So every time she was with another man, she did it as much as possible. 'Now,' she said, pulling her head away, 'let's tap into that anger. Tell me about a woman who hurt or rejected you. It doesn't have to be Louise.'

I could tell he didn't want to talk just then, but he played along. They sat on the bed and he thought for a moment. His face darkened and he spoke in short, staccato sentences. 'I had this girlfriend. She was called Jackie. She was studying German. Every couple of months, she went off to Germany to practice the language. At least, that's what she said. I found out later she was two-timing me. Some guy called Reiner.'

This must have happened a long time ago, but he still seemed upset about it. I wasn't sure we should be using it as part of an erotic scenario. Such considerations didn't bother Tina, though. Lying down, she said, 'Oh, I know Jackie. We often talk about you.'

I was fairly sure Tina had never heard of Jackie before. Nathan probably was too, but he asked in a menacing voice, 'What does she say?'

'She says what a turn-on it was, leaving you at the airport—the good little boyfriend who was going to stay faithful, while she went off to have fun with her German lover. On the plane, she felt her longing for him grow. By the time he met her at the other end, she was ready to burst. They couldn't wait until they got to his place. They had to pull the car over so he could fuck her on the back seat. And even now, she is so hot for him. She's always talking about how big and strong he was. Six foot two with blond hair and huge muscles. And the way she goes on about his cock! He was so much bigger and better than you. He fucked her longer and harder. He *always* made her cum. She never had to fake it with him the way she did with you.' She glanced up to see what effect this was having. Seeing his red face and hearing his rapid breathing, she smiled, but wanted to change the direction of his anger. 'And when she tells me all about it, I ….' Putting her hand between her legs, she rubbed her clit with urgent, jabbing fingers. 'I hear that this woman made a fool of you and … it turns me on so much.'

It worked. With an animal snarl, he leapt on her. 'Put my cock inside you, bitch.'

She grabbed his cock and his face contorted as she dug her fingernails into the tender skin. She stuffed his cock into her cunt and lay back. As he moved inside her, she raked his back with her nails, leaving scarlet wheals on his skin. This made him ram his cock into her even harder. I could see he was trying to make sex *painful* for Tina. It was deeply disturbing, but my cock was so hard I had to unzip my trousers and let it out. I rubbed it a little, but made sure I didn't cum. This would be impossible to watch if I wasn't turned on.

Tina moved her hands round to his chest and dragged her nails down his pecs. His response was to slap her left breast. He moved his chest closer to hers. I suspect he was trying to trap her hands so she couldn't scratch him anymore. Grabbing a handful of her hair, he pulled it as he fucked her. His hair was too short for her to answer in kind, so she pulled her hand from under his chest and gave him a ringing smack across the face. This made him cry out with rage and lust, but I think he wanted to get out of range. Keeping his cock inside her, he knelt up and maneuvered Tina's right foot onto his left shoulder. This changed the angle of his thrusts and allowed his cock to hit a different part of her cunt. 'Not so hard, you're hurting me,' she said.

He knew by now she didn't mean it and took it as a call for him to pound her as hard as he could. Now she couldn't touch him, she used words to hurt him. Sneering, she said, 'You're not the best I've ever had—not by a long way.'

'You're not that great, either,' he replied.

'Fuck off, I'm the best.'

'No,' he said, 'Louise is better than you.'

'How?' she asked.

'She's tighter than you. Your cunt's too wide.' She preferred to talk about her "pussy" and wouldn't have allowed me to use the c word, but it seemed he could do anything and it would turn her on. 'You've had too many cocks inside it. You've been putting out like the dirty whore you are.'

Her mouth was wide open and her breathing was getting faster. I knew what that meant, and I'm fairly sure he did too. His expression was one I'd seen on other men's faces while they were with my wife. He was trying to keep going until she came. Tina's body tensed. She was very close. 'Dirty little slut,' he said, fiercely. This was enough to push her over the edge. She came with a shout. On hearing that, he relaxed and groaned as he came inside her.

'Let me feel it pumping into me,' she said. After a moment, he pulled out and sat on the edge of the bed. She couldn't speak immediately. Raising her head to look at him, she said, 'That was fucking intense.' He didn't answer, so she turned to me. 'What do you say to Nathan?'

This was one of the moments when I regretted doing this with a friend. Nathan and I had played pool together. We'd chatted many times in bars, restaurants, and at barbecues. We'd always interacted as equals. And now I had to look him in the eye and say, 'Thank you for fucking my wife.'

'And?' prompted Tina.

'And for doing it better than I ever could.'

Nathan, to his credit, didn't gloat. I think he found this part as embarrassing as I did. Tina gave me a searching look. I didn't know immediately what it meant. I understood when she reached for a wad of Kleenex and wiped her cunt. She'd been asking herself if she should make me eat Nathan's cum out of her, but decided I'd had enough for the moment.

Nathan had the dazed look of someone who'd been in an accident. I guessed he was suffering from domdrop—or subdrop, I couldn't be sure which. Although they'd planned a weekend of Nathan dominating Tina, it was looking like two-way traffic with Tina giving as good as she got. And now it was Tina who offered the aftercare. She moved across the bed to give him room and extended her right arm toward him. 'Come here,' she said. He lay down and she put her arm around him.

'Was it okay?' he asked, in a scared voice.

'You did great, honey,' she said. 'Better than anything we discussed. Best fuck of my life.' I suspected this wasn't true and I wasn't sure if her intention was to reassure him or have a dig at me.

'I'm glad,' he said, sounding more content. She held him tight. As his body relaxed, his breathing deepened and turned into snores.

Tina looked up at me. 'We haven't had anything to eat, yet. I'm hungry. I'll give him a couple of minutes to settle and then I'll join you.'

I went into the kitchen and rummaged through the boxes of food we'd bought. I found eggs, onions, and mushrooms, so I thought I could rustle up an omelet. I went back to the bedroom to see if this was all right with Tina, and found she'd fallen asleep. I couldn't be bothered to cook just for myself, so I put the food in the fridge. If I'd been a rookie cuckold, I'd have slept on the couch. But experience had taught me ways of curling myself around Tina when she was sleeping next to another man.

They were both still naked. Nevertheless, I took my pajamas out of my bag and changed into them. Without waking them, I got onto the bed, switched off the bedside lamp, and spooned my wife while she held her lover in her arms.

Chapter Eight

~

ON SATURDAY MORNING, I found I'd been pushed into a six inch wide space on the left of the bed and was barely hanging on. Nathan was awake. He nodded at me, then turned back to Tina, who was opening her eyes. 'Morning,' she said.

He didn't say anything but took her hand and placed it on his cock. Feeling how hard he was, she smiled. He climbed on top of her and she fed his cock into her cunt. I was surprised he didn't move inside her. Instead, he asked, 'What do you want to do today? We can't stay in bed all weekend.'

She gave a little pout. 'We can at least try.'

He chuckled, but said, 'There's a leisure complex attached to the hotel. I thought we'd play tennis this morning.'

'I don't play,' she said, 'but Rob's always up for a game.'

'And there's a restaurant and cocktail bar where we can have lunch.'

Grinning, she said, 'Now you're talking. With a couple of banana daiquiris inside me, you might just get lucky.' I couldn't believe that, after only one day, it felt so natural for him to be inside my wife. Her cunt was just a convenient place to keep his dick while they planned their day. 'If we're out all morning, you'd better give me something to keep me going until we get back.'

This time, they didn't scratch or slap each other; nor did they say anything. But there was still something angry in the way they fucked. I could tell from her sharp intake of breath as he started to move that her cunt was still sore from the night before. He realized it too and thrust into her even harder. Tina's eyes were hard and her lips tight as she looked up at him. She kept this expression right up until the moment when her mouth opened, her eyes closed and she came. He must have cum at the same time, because he pulled out immediately. Tina said, 'Rob, you know what to do.'

I hadn't expected to get away with it twice. Nathan stood beside the bed as I knelt between my wife's legs and ate another man's cum out of her cunt. It was his second time in eight hours, so there wasn't too much of it. As always, I enjoyed Tina's moans of pleasure as I licked her.

When she was clean, I straightened up and she looked at Nathan. 'There's cum and pussy juice on your cock,' she told him.

'Yes,' he said. 'I was hoping *you* were going to clean *me* now.'

She gave me her wicked look. 'Rob, why don't you—?'

'No!' I said.

I must have sounded emphatic enough, because she turned to Nathan and said, 'Wipe it on Rob's pajamas.' He used the bottom of my pajama jacket to clean his cock. I knew Tina would have liked to see him gazing at me with contempt as he did it, but he was too embarrassed to meet my eye and looked down at what he was doing. When he'd finished, Tina said, 'Wear those stains with pride, Rob. If I think you've been washing them off … well, there's toothpaste in the bathroom.' If Nathan knew the significance of this, he didn't show it.

They headed off to the bathroom together. It seemed the no-privacy rule was still in force. I went into the kitchen and made breakfast. Half an hour later, we walked over to another part of the sprawling hotel grounds. We found a low-roofed square clubhouse where people were drinking coffee or preparing to play golf. Next to it were two tennis courts surrounded by high cypress hedges. It was a sunny November morning—not too cold—a good day for tennis. If I'd known we were going to play, I'd have brought my own gear. As it was, I had to hire an unfamiliar racket. Even so, I knew I was going to win easily as soon as the knock-up started. The first ball from Nathan came over the net fast, but didn't have enough power to trouble me. And it came straight to my hitting zone. There was no top spin to make it rear up awkwardly to shoulder height. When the game began, I sent my first two serves flying past him. He managed to return the third one, but it dropped tamely inside the service line and I stepped in for an easy cross-court winner. His shoulders drooped as he realized he didn't have a chance. I even had the pleasure of easing up and letting him win a couple of games. In this respect, anyway, I was the physically superior one.

Tina sat on the sidelines, watching us. After the match was over, she gave me a hug and said, 'You played well.'

She looked around. The hedges protected us from prying eyes, and she put her hand down Nathan's shorts. 'I need to feel those huge balls of yours.' She made a face of mock disgust. 'They're all sweaty.'

'This afternoon, you're going to lick them clean,' he said.

She moaned with desire at this prospect. Suddenly, I didn't feel so much of a winner.

After lunch and a couple of cocktails, we walked back to the cottage. As the front door closed behind us, Tina asked, a little nervously, 'Did you … bring the cane?'

'Of course,' replied Nathan.

'Do you … want to put it to good use?'

He went out to his car and came back with a bulging plastic bag and a cane. It was a simple length of bamboo, suggesting he'd found a trip to the garden center more convenient than one to the sex shop. He handed Tina the bag, and in his best dominant voice said, 'Go into the bedroom and put this on. Call me when you're ready.'

Tina took the bag into the bedroom. I wondered how he wanted her to dress. Naughty schoolgirl? Sexy nurse? Bad cop? Ten minutes later, she called his name and we went into the bedroom to find her wearing a gray trouser suit with a white blouse and black framed glasses. Slutty secretary—I hadn't thought of that one. Nathan turned to me and said, 'Rob, undress.'

This was a surprise. I'd expected all his attention to be focused on her. The thought of Nathan seeing me naked worried me. I knew this was irrational. Tina's lovers had seen my body before. Unfavorable comparisons with the bull were part of being a cuckold. But Nathan was a friend. I didn't see how a friendship could survive without a certain mutual respect. And how would Nathan ever respect me again if I stood in front of him naked, so he could ridicule me? I wanted to say, 'Look, this whole thing's a mistake. Trying this with a friend is insane. Let's have a normal weekend of playing tennis, drinking cocktails, and chatting.' I looked at Tina, hoping she was thinking the same thing, but she nodded at me, showing that she wanted me to do what he said. I found myself taking my clothes off. I stood in front of them, with what I hoped was a look of quiet defiance. Nathan looked at me, but didn't show any contempt. I wasn't erect, but there was enough blood in my cock for it to be a reasonable size. He told me to sit on the green wicker chair in the corner. As I did, I noticed something glinting on the floor behind me. Nathan stood behind the chair. He grabbed my right arm and locked a handcuff around my wrist. Soon, both my hands were restrained behind my back. When he was sure I couldn't move, he turned back to Tina. 'I've been disappointed with your work, recently,' he said.

Looking at the floor in shame, she murmured, 'I'll try to do better in future.'

'I'll have to make sure you do. Kneel. Hands.'

Tina knelt and held her hands in front of her, palms up. Standing beside her, he swished the cane through the air a couple of times. He raised it above his head and brought it down on her hands with a sharp crack. Tina said, 'Ow!' I remembered what Charlotte had said about watching the eyes. I saw pain in Tina's face, but not the arousal that normally went with it. Nathan wasn't familiar enough with her reactions to notice this.

'Your last report was not completed on time and had several major errors in it,' he said, caning her hands again—slightly harder this time.

'*Marquis*,' said Tina, lowering her hands and rubbing the palms against her trousers.

'What's the matter?' he asked, looking concerned.

'It's okay. I don't want you to stop caning me, but can we stop pretending you're my boss? It's making me think of David, my real boss. And he does not turn me on.'

'Sorry,' he said.

'Don't be. You weren't to know. And also my hands aren't sexy.'

'I beg to differ,' I said.

They looked at me as if the chained man in the corner shouldn't be voicing an opinion, but Nathan said, 'So do I.'

'Thanks, guys,' she said, with a little smile. 'I mean they're not erogenous zones. These, on the other hand ....' Unbuttoning the white blouse, she showed him she wasn't wearing anything underneath. She looked up at him and said, 'Don't pretend to be anyone else. It's you I'm interested in. I want to tap in to *Nathan's* anger.' She paused for a second. 'You know, I really enjoyed watching Rob beat at you at tennis. You're a fucking loser. But ... I knew that already. Louise told me. It's why she never wants your help with anything. She knows you'll only fuck it all up.' Nathan's face tightened as he became more annoyed. Tina pushed her chest forward. He swung the cane and landed it across both her breasts. The sound was duller this time, more a thump than a crack. It left a thick red line across her tits. Tina moaned and closed her eyes. 'That's a real caning,' she said. He gave her breasts five more strokes of the cane. By the time he'd finished, they were covered with crisscrossed red lines and purple bruises. She stood up and gazed at me with an evil look on her face. 'You know, Rob, you beat Nathan earlier, so now it's only fair ....' My first thought was that I must refuse. This was not what I'd signed up for. All I needed was another unequivocal *No!* Tina must have seen this in my face, because she said, 'Nathan, can you give me a moment with my husband?'

He went out. Tina sat on my knee and kissed me. It was a passionate kiss, her tongue playing against mine. 'You love to turn me on, don't you, Rob?'

Before I could answer, her lips were on mine again. All I managed was an, 'Mm-mm,' of assent.

'I want to see this, Rob. Don't think of it as doing something with a man. Look on it as blowing your wife's mind. I'll be right beside you. You can look at my body while it's happening. You'll be so turned on you won't even notice the pain.' I found this hard to believe, but Tina's thigh was against my cock. Her freshly caned breasts were right in front of me. It was impossible to say no under these circumstances. She realized this and called to Nathan.

He came in and unlocked the handcuffs. I rubbed my wrists. 'On the bed,' he told me.

'Face down,' added Tina.

I lay on the bed and took a moment to enjoy the comfort, knowing it would soon be shattered. I thought of stopping the scene. We'd never discussed *my* use of the word, *Marquis*, but I didn't see why it shouldn't work. I kept quiet, though. A strange, perverse part of me wanted this to happen. Tina crouched by the side of the bed, directly in my eye line. 'Look at my tits, Rob,' she said. 'They're a mess from Nathan's cane. I want you to feel what I felt. He's only hurting you to turn *me* on. It's all about sex. And remember what Charlotte said. Sex has the power to turn pain into pleasure.'

Nathan walked up to the bed and stood on the other side of it. I heard the noise of the cane moving through the air like it was a long distance away—something which didn't affect me.

When it struck my butt cheeks, what I felt wasn't a sting but a bruising pain which made me sick. My lips formed the letter M. But I forced myself to focus on Tina's breasts. As I watched, she pressed her fingers into the most livid bruise and moaned. If she could take the pain, then so could I. He caned me again, not so hard this time. Tina wasn't satisfied. 'Come on, Nathan, you can do better than that. Or is this something else you're going to fuck up? Rob said he loved beating you at tennis, completely humiliating you.' I heard the grunt of Nathan's breath as he brought the cane down as hard as he could. I tried to scream but couldn't find my voice. It came out as a gasp. My ass felt like it would catch fire at any moment. 'Turn over,' said Tina. I rolled onto my back. I didn't know what was going to happen, but I wanted my butt out of the firing line. 'Let's see those balls of yours,' said Tina. With trepidation, I took my cock in my right hand and pulled it toward my belly button. 'His balls are pathetic, aren't they, Nathan?'

'Smaller than mine,' he said.

'Show me what you think of them.'

I felt the cane whooshing past my hand. It landed across both my balls. It was the most severe pain I'd ever felt. My body jackknifed defensively and I put my hands to my crotch. I shut my eyes but couldn't stop the tears. At that moment, I couldn't imagine why people thought pain was erotic. Then I opened my eyes and saw my wife with her right hand rubbing her clit, her left tugging hard on her left nipple, and her face an open-mouthed mask of sadistic ecstasy. This was enough to send a jolt of sex through my body and counteract the agony.

'You have to do that again,' she told Nathan, in a voice hoarse with desire. I knew I couldn't take any more at that moment, so I was relieved to hear her add, 'Some time. But, right now, I badly need to be fucked.' After what I'd been through, I thought *I'd* earned the right to have sex with my wife. I didn't know if I *could* do anything, but it would have been nice to be asked. Instead, Tina stood up and pointed me back to my corner. Gingerly, I got off the bed and hobbled to the chair. I cried out as my buttocks touched the rough wicker. Picking up the handcuffs, Tina secured my hands behind my back again. 'Look at Rob,' she told Nathan, laughing. 'Poor little cucky with his aching ass and balls. And he can't even touch himself to ease the pain.'

'I wouldn't want to be him,' he said.

I thought they'd start fucking without delay. But, instead, she looked at me for a while longer, and asked him, 'Does Louise find Rob attractive?'

I didn't know where this question had come from, but it seemed Nathan had been expecting it. His response sounded prepared. 'None of our friends do. The main topic of conversation is how someone like Rob snagged a girl like you.'

In fairness, this was a question I'd asked myself many times. But I wasn't going to admit that now. 'I felt sorry for him,' said Tina.

'I can see why,' he replied.

I didn't know if they wanted a reaction from me. Was I supposed to get angry … or upset? Tina had said she wanted a mindfuck element to her BDSM relationship. I didn't realize it was *my* mind she wanted to fuck with. I kept calm by telling myself it wasn't true. You might date someone for a short time because you felt sorry for him, but you wouldn't marry him and stay with him for seventeen years. Tina continued, 'I met him at college, where he was dating this skank called Deborah.'

'The best he could get,' said Nathan.

'You want to hear something funny?' she asked.

Hello! Didn't you say you badly needed to be fucked? What's with the comic anecdotes?

'He lost his virginity to her,' she said.

He gave me a sympathetic look. 'Dude? You lost it to the college tramp?'

I didn't say anything. Deborah was an innocent party in all this. I don't think I was ever in love with her, but I was fond of her, and grateful to her for being my first. I didn't like hearing her bad-mouthed like this.

'She told me he was already cumming before he was fully inside her,' said Tina. 'In and out in less than a second. Very economical.'

Firstly, I'd managed to thrust into Deborah ten times before I came. I'd always thought that quite impressive for a man's first time. And secondly, Deborah and Tina hardly knew each other and I was fairly sure they'd never discussed me.

'I'm friends with Deborah on Facebook,' said Tina. 'We love swapping stories about times Rob couldn't get it up or came too soon.'

I *knew* this was a lie, for the simple reason that Tina would have teased me about it before.

'Louise says Rob makes women uncomfortable,' said Nathan.

Tina nodded as if she wasn't surprised. 'Cuckolds always do. It's creepy enough if a man looks at a woman thinking, "I want to fuck you." But imagine a guy thinking, "I'd love to watch another man fucking you." ' She shuddered.

'So why do you stay with him?' asked Nathan.

'What can I tell you? A cuckoldress needs a cuckold.'

'But wouldn't you prefer to have a man who wouldn't share you with anyone, who could give you what you wanted?'

'Now, that's the best idea I've heard in a long time,' she said. Finally, she lay on the bed and said, 'My pussy's nearly as sore as Rob's balls, so be gentle with me.'

By now, he knew what this meant. Getting on top of her, he stuck his cock inside her. He fucked her hard. After everything she'd seen and done, it took her less than a minute to cum from the relentless action of his cock. As soon as she'd finished, he thrust into my wife three more times and shot his load into her.

As soon as he pulled out, he reached into a bag next to the bed and took out a tube of lotion, which he rubbed gently onto Tina's breasts. 'Nice and cool,' she said, contentedly.

'Was it okay?' he asked, again.

'Perfect,' she replied. 'I sure know I've been caned. But it wasn't unbearable.'

I gave an involuntary snort. I hadn't been so lucky. They both looked round at me. 'Maybe you should give your husband something,' he said. 'But hands only.'

Tina got off the bed and knelt in front of the chair. 'Blocked or ruined?' she asked.

'My balls are ready to burst, so blocked would be torture,' I said.

'We'll go with that, then.' She put her right hand around my cock and pulled it hard.

I thought I would start cumming immediately, but she pulled it five times, before I felt myself approaching the point of no return. 'Now!' I said.

She squeezed my cock as hard as she could. The head of my cock was a royal purple. I managed to stop myself from screaming, but I let out a deep groan of pain. Tina didn't relax her grip. Only when she was sure the moment had passed and I wasn't going to cum did she move her hand away.

'Nathan and I are going into the kitchen for a drink now,' she said. 'We'll leave you to think through everything that's happened.'

'That's your idea of aftercare, is it?' I asked.

She didn't say any more, but switched off the light. They went out, closing the door behind them. I was naked, handcuffed to a chair, in the dark. I had watched as my wife was caned and fucked. I'd experienced the worst physical pain of my life. And my cock and balls were desperate for relief. Tina had done everything possible to make my pain and frustration even worse. Nevertheless, I felt strangely proud of myself, as if I'd completed Special Forces training or gotten through a prison sentence. I'd taken everything cuckoldry had thrown at me, and I'd survived.

Chapter Nine

~

THE NEXT MORNING, THE hotel delivered breakfast and the Sunday papers to our cottage. Tina and Nathan were sitting up in bed. They were both naked. I was the only one who had bothered dressing and was sitting on my green wicker chair with a paper on the floor in front of me. My balls were still tender and I winced whenever I moved, but at least there was no swelling. The day before, Tina had released me from the handcuffs after ten minutes, but I hadn't jerked off. The post-orgasmic blues would have given me the worst ever case of *cuckdrop*. We'd had a normal evening. There was a widescreen TV in the lounge. We'd eaten omelets and watched movies until it was time for bed.

Nathan's phone beeped. He looked at the screen for a couple of minutes, but then casually tossed the phone aside with the words, 'I'll read it later.' He went back to his breakfast.

As I finished my orange juice, I contemplated the scene in the bed. It shouldn't have been too distressing—especially when compared with what had happened the day before. The covers had fallen to expose Tina's breasts. Most wives would have been embarrassed, but she was a *hot* wife and we were used to her showing her body in front of other men. Tina and Nathan weren't touching each other but what they *were* doing seemed more intimate than physical contact. They were enjoying breakfast in bed together. He was trying to be healthy and had ordered the fruit salad. She had a plate of pancakes and syrup, but occasionally reached across with her fork to steal a chunk of mango from his bowl. I'd seen this sort of closeness before. It had developed between Tina and Adam. To a lesser extent, it had happened with Steve. However much Tina said she could separate emotional attachment from sexual attraction, the two kept overlapping. It was hard for her to invite a man into her bed with an access-all-areas pass to her body and not develop feelings for him.

Nathan finished the fruit salad and placed his bowl on the bedside table. He stayed in bed, eyeing Tina impatiently. She knew he was waiting for her to put down her plate, but she enjoyed teasing him, picking up tiny fragments of pancake until her plate was spotless. When she finally put it aside and turned to face him, they didn't say anything. Grabbing her shoulders, he pushed her onto the bed and got on top of her. The red marks on her breasts had faded, but she still had several bruises. A cruel look came into his eyes as he grabbed her tits and squeezed them hard. Tina threw back her head and screamed. This time, it looked like the perfect mix of pain and pleasure. 'You bastard,' she said in a low voice. 'Get inside me. *Now!*'

I saw movement under the covers. When he flinched, I guessed that she'd grabbed his cock harder than necessary. His expression soon changed to one of ecstasy and I knew she'd put his cock inside her. He fucked her hard. She scratched his back and he responded by slapping her tits and twisting her nipples. After a few minutes, though, they slowed down. He put his arms around her and kissed her. Gazing into her eyes, he moved with a slow, steady rhythm until her body went rigid and she came with a sigh. He thrust into her for another two minutes until he closed his eyes, tensed his muscles for a second, and then relaxed. I knew he'd cum inside her.

He didn't move. They lay in each other's arms for a long time. I thought he was probably still inside her. 'Oh, Tina,' he said, at last.

'You got my name right—well done,' she replied, with a smile.

'It's different with you.'

'In what way?'

'I realize now … everything I've done with other people was like cut-for-TV sex. With you, it's uncensored … stronger. It's *better* with you.' He rolled off her and onto his side. Looking at her intently, he said, 'It's not enough.'

'What do you mean?'

'One weekend with you. This can't be the end.'

'I think we're free next weekend,' said Tina. 'We could do this all over again.'

Shaking his head, he said, 'I want you to come back with me to my apartment.'

'And what do you want to do with me in your apartment?' she asked, coquettishly.

There was no teasing in his reply. His voice was serious as he said, 'I want to fuck you. I'm going to wake up and fuck you before work. During my lunch break, I'm going to find you and fuck you. In the evening, I'm going to fuck you over the kitchen table, on the couch, in the shower, on the floor. Then I'm going to take you to bed and fuck you to sleep.'

Breathing heavily, she said, 'Sounds like a good plan. But … why don't you come home with us?'

He cast a glance at me and said, 'I want some time with just the two of us.'

She was silent for a moment, her eyes burning into his. Slowly, she turned her head and said, 'I think I'm going home with Nathan. Sorry, Rob.'

I looked back at her and said quietly, 'You wanted me to look after you.'

Turning back to Nathan, she asked him, 'You can look after me, can't you, babe?'

He nodded. 'After I fuck you, I'll be there to hold and soothe you.'

'One weekend and you're moving in together,' I said, in a tone more resigned than incredulous.

'I'm going to try it, at least,' she said.

I looked in her eyes and saw that infuriating complacency again. She was safe in her belief that she could go off with Nathan and, if it didn't work out, she could come back to me. She wasn't risking anything because I would always be there as her safety net.

Nathan reached for his phone. 'That message was from Louise. She reckons we might still be able to make it. She wants me to go round there and talk.' He looked at Tina. 'But there's no way I can go back to her. Not now I know what it's *really* like. I'm texting Louise right now. I'm going to tell her everything.'

I held up a restraining hand. 'Nathan, this is what teenagers do: one date and they declare undying love.'

He waved away my concerns. 'I know what I'm doing.'

He spent a couple of minutes jabbing the screen of his phone. He handed it to Tina and she read, 'Hi Louise. Thanks for your message but talking would be pointless. I've found someone else. Someone who needs me. It's Tina. You take care of yourself. Goodbye.'

'I think that should do it, don't you?' said Nathan, in a self-satisfied way.

'Not much room for doubt there,' she agreed.

I shook my head. 'You're not going along with this, are you, Tina?'

She put her arm around his shoulders. 'Maybe I want this man all to myself.'

'Nathan,' I said, sharply, 'you and Louise have been together close on twenty years. Don't you think she deserves better than this?'

Tina butted in, 'If it were me, I'd want to know.'

Nathan agreed. 'Best to make a clean break—less painful in the long run.'

'At least have the balls to say it to her face. No one should get news like this by text.'

'It's the modern world,' he said, dismissively. 'Text, email, face-to-face—no difference anymore.'

'You are going to wake up tomorrow and you won't believe what an asshole you've been.'

Tina gave me an especially nasty version of her wicked look. 'He's going to wake up tomorrow with me in bed next to him. Naked and horny. The only thing he won't believe is his luck.'

He took his phone back from Tina and pressed the send button with a defiant glare in my direction. 'That's that!' he said.

'Yes, it is,' said Tina. 'You're a free man, now.'

'Does it make me less desirable?' he asked.

She responded by grabbing the back of his head and kissing him. She pushed her tongue into his mouth. 'See how repulsive I find you now,' she said, with a grin. 'Did I make you split up with your wife?'

'Yes, you did.'

'Does that make me a heartless bitch?'

'Given that Louise is your friend, I'd say yes it does.'

'What do you do to heartless bitches?'

He demonstrated by flipping her onto her front and pulling down the bedclothes to expose her ass. He supported himself on his right elbow as he spanked her with his left hand. It wasn't as strong as his right, but he didn't hold back, smacking her as hard as he could. Smiling, she rested her head on the pillow.

Despite this going on in front of me, I was thinking of Louise. She'd be angry at Nathan and Tina, and maybe at me if she discovered my complicity. And if she couldn't take revenge on any of us, she might ....

It's amazing how quickly you can move when you know exactly what you have to do. Ignoring the complaints from my balls, I jumped up, put my coat on, made sure my car keys were in the pocket, and went out. Nathan had finished spanking

Tina and was fucking her from behind. I doubt if they even noticed me leaving.

I left the cottage, got into the car, and drove the sixty miles to Louise's place. It says something about my priorities that my wife had announced she was going home with another man, and what I cared about most was my dog.

Boris greeted me with his usual enthusiasm. Louise didn't look like she'd received devastating news. Nor did she look too surprised to see me. We'd arranged to pick Boris up on Sunday afternoon. I was only a few hours earlier than expected. 'Is Tina with you?' she asked.

I shook my head and said, 'She's tied up,' which might have been true, for all I knew. 'How are you?' I asked, watching her closely.

'Bearing up,' she said.

'Have you … heard from Nathan?' I asked.

'Not in a while,' she said, sadly. 'I texted him this morning but he hasn't gotten back to me yet.'

I felt sorry for her and wondered if I should tell her what was happening. But, I reflected, it didn't have much to do with me. It was between Nathan, Louise, and Tina. I couldn't see a place for me in that triangle. I gave her a longer hug than normal—partly to thank her, but mainly out of sympathy for the shit heading her way. Boris jumped into the back of the car. Breathing a huge sigh of relief, I drove him home.

I put a load of washing into the machine. I was particularly keen to wash my pajamas. Going into the den, I sat on the couch. Turning on the TV, I told Boris, 'Let's watch some sports.' But Boris didn't want to watch sports. He put his chin on my knee and looked up at me with big eyes. 'Nothing wrong with this, buddy,' I reminded him. 'Remember when I adopted you … sorry, when *you* adopted *me*, it was just the two of us. It was fine.' His expression told me he didn't like the idea of living in a bachelor pad. 'You're right,' I said, patting his head. 'We have to get her back.'

I didn't mean Tina.

Chapter Ten

~

Going into the teachers' lounge on Monday morning, I found Danielle. She looked up with the amused smirk she always wore when she saw me. I was usually embarrassed when I ran into her at work and she found this entertaining. But this morning, she was the person I wanted to see and I sat beside her. 'How was your weekend?' I asked.

She was proud of her idiomatic English and answered, 'Pretty chilled.'

'Danielle ….'

'Rob?'

Taking a deep breath, I said, 'Danielle, it's fair to say I've treated you badly.'

She raised her eyebrows. 'News to me.'

'Nice of you to say that, but, it's true. You were there for me when I split from my wife. But when I was back with her, I rejected you.'

She gave a broad, Gallic shrug and said, 'The game of love is not easy to play.'

'Ain't that the truth? But it was a shitty way to treat a friend, so I'll understand if you send me away with a flea in my ear.'

She frowned. 'I don't know this expression.'

'If you tell me to fuck off.'

'This, I understand. What do you want to ask me?'

When I'd finished explaining my idea, I saw her mind working as she tried to find the right words. I feared she was thinking up some colorful way of telling me to fuck off. But she grinned and said, 'Sounds like a blast.'

ON SATURDAY EVENING, I took my tuxedo out of the wardrobe. I felt sad as I moved Tina's clothes out of the way. I was surprised she hadn't needed any of them during the week, but maybe Nathan had taken his new girl shopping. Boris watched as I pressed my suit trousers and put them on. He knew when I got dressed up, he spent time alone. After I'd fastened my bow tie, I stroked his head and said, 'Wish me luck, buddy.'

I drove over to Danielle's apartment at eight o'clock. She was waiting outside her building. As I pulled over, I asked myself again why someone who looked like her had ever given me the time of day. She had shoulder-length black hair, dark brown eyes, and olive skin. She was dressed in a skintight black top with bare shoulders. The outfit was completed with black ski pants and patent leather boots. 'You look great,' I said, as she got into the car.

'You too,' she replied. 'You could walk straight into the Casino Le Croisette.'

'They'd throw me out when I asked where the penny slots were.' Driving off, I said, 'I apologize in advance for any strange things you see tonight.'

'I have seen many things in my life.'

'I doubt if you've seen anything like Pandora's Box.'

'Don't be too sure. I am not exactly a virgin in these matters.'

I parked the car in a small lot two streets away from the club. I was nervous as we stepped into the dark tunnel and I saw the black door. Going into the club without Charlotte reminded me of the first time I'd gone to the movies without my mom. Did I know the right things to do and say in order to get in? I banged on the door and was glad to see a familiar face when it opened. 'Hey, Derek, how are you?' I said, trying to sound like we were old friends.

'Hello,' was his only reply. I'm not sure he recognized me, but he looked us over and waved us toward the desk where we signed in. I paid for both of us and we went downstairs.

Danielle wrinkled her nose as she smelled the damp. 'Feeling sexy yet?' I asked. We were already wearing our outfits for the evening, so we didn't have to change but I went to the men's room to leave my coat and bag. I took Danielle into the bar area. The club was more crowded than last time. All the tables at the bar were occupied. The bench was in the middle of the floor, but no one was near it. Danielle calmly watched the people in their various costumes. She seemed comfortable in this place. Even so, I didn't know what she'd make of the activities in the dungeon and wanted to spare her those—at least for the moment. 'Guess what I forgot to do when I was in the bathroom,' I told her. 'Can you get us a drink? I'll be back in a minute.' I offered her some money, but she waved it away.

'I'll see if these people know anything about brandy,' she said, and headed to the bar.

I went through the door and down the steps.

There wasn't much going on in the dungeon. An old man was lying on a rug, while a younger woman in a nurse's uniform spanked him. She looked bored. He wasn't showing many signs of pleasure, either. They looked like they couldn't remember *why* they did this: it was simply a pattern they'd fallen into. In another part of the room, two people were having more fun. A girl in a studded collar was chasing a tennis ball thrown by her master. If she brought it back quickly enough and sat nicely at his feet, he gave her a chocolate. They were both grinning happily, enjoying the absurdity of what they were doing.

I went back upstairs. As soon as I opened the door to the bar area, I saw her—face down on the bench. She was wearing a see-through white negligee. Natalie, in a tight purple leather dress, stood at the side of the bench. She was whipping Charlotte with a five-tailed flogger. I stood directly in front of Charlotte, willing her to look up. Eventually, she did and I saw her eyes. I immediately read their message. They were the eyes of one who had been taken somewhere she didn't want to go. There was something else I noticed, as well. Charlotte normally had bright, inquisitive eyes. But now they were dull and lifeless.

I held up my pointing finger, hoping she'd interpret it as *I'll be back in one minute*. She didn't react. I hadn't seen any sign that she even knew who I was. I went to the bar. It was no surprise that Danielle had attracted attention, looking the way she did. She was talking in rapid French to a bare-chested man in shiny black latex trousers. 'Rob, this is Bruno,' she said, as I came up to them.

'Nice to meet you,' I said. I didn't know how good his English was, so I spoke in the slow, clear voice I used for teaching. 'I know we've only just met, Bruno, but could I ask a favor?'

'Bruno is submissive,' said Danielle. 'You don't have to *ask*. You can *tell* him what to do.'

I gave him crisp instructions. I didn't threaten punishment if he didn't carry them out, for fear he'd fail deliberately. But I promised him Master Rob would be happy if he performed his task successfully. I jerked my thumb toward the door of the men's room, and he scurried off to do my bidding.

I explained the rest of my plan to Danielle, and hoped she could follow what I was saying. The language of BDSM clubs was probably not included in her school English lessons.

She took a deep breath and stepped into the middle of the floor. Speaking with a stronger accent than usual, she announced, 'I am Mistress Danielle. I am a French dominatrix.' This immediately sparked interest in those watching. The French have always had a reputation for their sophisticated sexiness. I think the people in the club wanted to see what Gallic flavor she'd bring to the proceedings. Natalie looked around and was obviously impressed by this beautiful woman. 'Mistress,' said Danielle, 'you look tired from punishing your slave. May I help you?'

Natalie looked delighted with this idea. Handing the flogger to Danielle, she said, 'Help yourself, mistress, and don't hold back. Anything you give her is a lot less than she deserves.'

Leaning down so her lips were close to Charlotte's left ear, Danielle said, 'I will make you pay for being such a dirty little slut.' She bent a little farther and whispered something I didn't hear. But if she used the line I'd given her, she said something like, 'I'm with Rob—we're going to get you out of here.'

Danielle stood up and started hitting Charlotte's butt with the flogger. After the fifth stroke, she said, 'It is not enough for a whore such as this.' She looked at Natalie. 'I think she must go to the dungeon. Do you agree?'

'Definitely!' said Natalie.

There was a cheer from the onlookers. Danielle pulled Charlotte roughly off the bench and marched her to the dungeon door. Natalie and most of the crowd were on the point of following. I had to buy Danielle some time. I knew what I had to do, even though it would annoy the people, some of whom had whips and canes. I ran up to Natalie and said, 'Punish me, Madame Toxic!'

The last time Natalie and I had met, she'd given me nothing more than a contemptuous glance, so I didn't think she'd remember me. And there was no recognition in her eyes as she looked at me open-mouthed, unable to believe a slave would be so bold. 'What do you think you're doing?' she asked.

'I have disrespected my mistress and she has sent me to Madame Toxic for punishment.'

She nodded as if that, at least, made sense. But she said, 'Out of my way. I might get to you later.'

'She said you are the best mistress in the club. Only you can give me what I deserve.' I hoped she'd want to stay to hear more compliments, but she pushed me aside and strode past me. With both hands, I caught hold of the leather straps at the back of her dress. Pulling her toward me, I planted my right foot into the back of her left knee. This caused her left leg to buckle and it was easy to manhandle her to the floor. Much as

I disliked Natalie, I didn't want to injure her, and I held onto her to make sure she had a soft landing. But, even if she wasn't physically hurt, she was furious at being treated like this in front of her admirers. 'What the hell are you doing, slave?' she demanded.

'Fuck you, Natalie,' I said.

I ran to the door and took the stairs to the dungeon three at a time. I didn't see Charlotte and Danielle. I hoped that meant things had gone according to plan. I went out through the fire exit and found them at the foot of some iron steps. The negligee was no protection against the night air and Charlotte was shivering. Bruno had completed his mission. He'd gone into the bathroom, picked up my coat along with the spare one I had in my bag, and placed them outside the door. I put on my coat and maneuvered Charlotte into the other one. I wrapped my arms around her to warm her up. She still showed no sign of recognizing me. 'Are you finished with me?' asked Danielle. 'I would like to spend more time with Bruno.'

I kissed her on both cheeks. 'Thank you so much for your help, Danielle. You're a better friend than I deserve.'

Danielle smiled and went back inside. As I led Charlotte up the steps, we were blocked by one of the bouncers. 'Emergency exit only!' he said, firmly. 'You have to leave by the main entrance.'

We couldn't go back inside for fear Natalie would see us. 'This *is* an emergency,' I said. 'I have to get her out of here.'

He stood his ground. 'If there was an emergency, I would know about it.'

This would have been a good moment for Charlotte to use her persuasive skills, but she was too out of it to say anything. I looked past the bouncer and saw the walled courtyard at the end of the tunnel. That meant the front door was right above us. 'Derek!' I shouted. 'Derek!'

I heard heavy footsteps on the ground above and Derek's substantial frame appeared at the top of the steps. 'What's going on?' he asked.

'It's Charlotte,' I called to him. 'She needs to get away from Natalie.'

'I've thought that for a long time,' he said. 'Okay, Tim, let them through.' Tim stood aside and we hurried past him. When we were at the top of the steps, Derek said, 'She doesn't look too good.'

'I think she's been drugged with something.'

He looked at me, sternly. 'You look after her, my friend, or I'll find you and give you a kicking.'

Charlotte was having trouble walking. Wanting to get her out of harm's way as quickly as possible, I picked her up. Tina had always been too large for me to carry. Even Boris was uncomfortably heavy. But Charlotte was just the right size. We passed a group of people enjoying a night out. One of the women looked concerned and asked, 'Is she okay?'

'It's her birthday,' I said. 'One too many cocktails, but she'll be fine in the morning.' The woman nodded and went after her friends.

I got to the car and laid Charlotte across the back seats. There was no way of putting a safety belt on her, so I took extra care, driving home.

I parked outside our gate and had a quick look up and down the street. I didn't want anyone to see me carrying a barely conscious woman into our house. No one was around, so I took Charlotte inside and sat her on the couch in the den. Boris realized something was wrong and didn't jump up at her. Instead, he sat by the couch and watched her anxiously. I went into the kitchen and made a large mug of strong coffee. I felt good about myself. I was making a habit of swooping in and saving the day. But it suddenly occurred to me that I might have done the wrong thing. I'd acted on my interpretation of a look from someone who was high. If Charlotte wanted to be free of Natalie, I'd saved her. If she didn't, I'd kidnapped her.

I went back into the den and, kneeling beside Boris, put the mug to Charlotte's lips. As she drank, she became more alert until she looked at me and smiled. 'Hi, sweetie,' she said, thickly. This was enough for Boris. I had to pull the mug out of the way as he put his front paws on the couch to lick her face. 'Hello, Boris,' she said. It was good she recognized him.

She drank all the coffee, but her eyes were still closing. I let her sleep for an hour while I watched TV with the sound muted. 'Rob …' said a voice from the couch.

'How you doing, Charlotte?' I asked, turning my head.

'Thank you,' she said. It was all I needed to know I'd done the right thing.

I should have let her rest some more, but there were things I wanted to ask. 'Why didn't you get in touch?'

'Natalie said she'd keep my phone in a safe place. I haven't seen it since I got with her.'

This led me to the most important question. 'Why on earth were you with her?'

She sighed deeply. 'Why does an addict keep going back to the drug? You know it's destroying you, but you can't stay away. I knew I was going to see her when we went to Pandora's Box. After all, there are other clubs we could have gone to. I thought I could handle it. It was like taking the drug one more time—to prove you're clean.'

'Talking of drugs, what were you on tonight?'

She shook her head. 'I've no idea. She mixed something into my beer and said it would make me enjoy the evening more.'

'And you drank it?'

'I've fallen into the habit of doing what she says.' She looked around the room, as if she thought someone might be hiding. 'Where's Tina?'

'She's gone off with Nathan. Apparently, they're together now.'

She made a face. 'Seriously? Him?'

I shrugged. 'Her choice.'

There was a silence and she looked at me. 'Why were you at the club tonight, Rob?'

'I came to find you.'

'Why?' she asked, with tears welling up.

'Because I love you, Charlotte.'

'Tina's the love of your life.'

'And Natalie's yours.'

'But right now, I don't want to be with the love of my life.' Looking away, she mumbled, 'I'd rather be with my friend.'

'So would I.'

She patted Boris's head and said, 'Maybe we can make our own little family—just the three of us.'

Charlotte and I went upstairs and took our clothes off. Whatever our relationship was or would be, there was no need for coyness between us. We got into bed and I put my arm around her, inhaling her distinctive mixture of perfume and sweat. There was a thump as Boris made a successful landing on the bed and his contented breathing told me he'd laid his head next to mine on the pillow.

I found myself asking, *What is a family?* When politicians talked about family values, they normally meant a wife, a husband, and a couple of kids. But times were changing and so were families. Two moms, two dads, no mom, no dad, no kids. Most of them seemed to do okay. But what about us—a cuckold, a lesbian, and a dog? It sounded more like the opening line of a joke than the make-up of a happy family.

I knew we were being almost as rash as Tina. She'd decided she wanted to be with Nathan after a single weekend. But here I was, considering a future with Charlotte, a girl I'd known for only a few weeks.

But as I lay there between Charlotte and Boris, I was enveloped by a warm feeling of being exactly where I was supposed to be.

ROB MATTHEWS WAS BORN in London. He divides his time between Britain and the United States. He's the author of the Cuckold Odyssey series: *Come Home With Us*, *I Can Do It Better*, *We Make Our Own Rules*, and *I'm the One You Need*. He's also written the stand-alone book, *Black and Blue - An Interracial Cuckold Tale*. Rob is currently working on two more interracial cuckold tales, *Talking Bull* and *Black Friday*. Both are coming soon from Fanny Press.

Follow Rob on Facebook and Twitter:

www.facebook.com/robertpatrickmatthews

@robandtina1